LODESTAR

ROCKET SHIP TO MARS

By Franklyn M. Branley

LODESTAR: ROCKET SHIP TO MARS

EXPERIMENTS IN THE PRINCIPLES OF SPACE TRAVEL

SOLAR ENERGY

THE NINE PLANETS

EXPERIMENTS IN SKY WATCHING

THE MOON: EARTH'S NATURAL SATELLITE

MARS: PLANET NUMBER FOUR

THE SUN: STAR NUMBER ONE

THE EARTH: PLANET NUMBER FOUR

MAN IN SPACE TO THE MOON

THE MILKY WAY: GALAXY NUMBER ONE

By Franklyn M. Branley and Nelson F. Beeler

EXPERIMENTS IN SCIENCE

EXPERIMENTS WITH ELECTRICITY

MORE EXPERIMENTS IN SCIENCE

EXPERIMENTS IN OPTICAL ILLUSION

EXPERIMENTS IN CHEMISTRY

EXPERIMENTS WITH AIRPLANE INSTRUMENTS

EXPERIMENTS WITH ATOMICS

EXPERIMENTS WITH A MICROSCOPE

EXPERIMENTS WITH LIGHT

LODESTAR

ROCKET SHIP TO MARS

THE RECORD OF THE FIRST OPERATION
SPONSORED BY THE FEDERAL COMMISSION
FOR INTERPLANETARY EXPLORATION,
JUNE 1, 1988

BY FRANKLYN M. BRANLEY

THOMAS Y. CROWELL COMPANY · NEW YORK

Designed by Maurice Serle Kaplan

Manufactured in the United States of America

ISBN 0-690-50443-8

9   10   11   12   13   14   15

To Dad

CONTENTS

AN AIR of excitement hung over the launching area. This spacious desert bowl, which covered ten square miles, was the focus of the eyes of the world on the morning of June 30, 1988. For many years, ever since the close of the second world war, scientists had been working in this bowl under the greatest secrecy to develop a man-carrying rocket that could reach outer space. After decades of preparation they had reached the moon, and this day would see man's first attempt to reach the other planets of his solar system.

Thousands of spectators, some well-wishers and some skeptics who came to criticize, lined the plateau that formed the rim of the bowl. None but the privileged were allowed inside. All others were kept out by a heavy radar screen which covered the bowl like an invisible dome. Hemispheres forty feet in diameter dotted the twelve miles of the rim like carefully placed mushrooms. Radar installations within each of these scanned the sky above the bowl, and blanketed an area forty miles in diameter.

Any plane venturing into this zone was intercepted by small, heavily armed, jet planes. The trespasser was warned to change his course. If he did not comply, the jets flew in close to the stranger and forced him to change course.

Security on the ground level was maintained by heavy radar beams which scanned the area between each dome, making a wall thirty feet high through which no one could pass without his presence being shown in a sensitive pickup. Squads of security officers, hand picked and highly trained, were strategically placed so they could reach any point around the rim or within the bowl in a matter of seconds.

The scores of workmen, stenographers, mechanics, and physicists within the area were free to move about. They had been working together for so long that they knew one another well, and the mutual friendships served as convenient but nevertheless vigilant checks on security.

The bowl was a natural depression very close to the geographic center of the great desert of southwestern United States. The activities were carried out here because the desert was removed from population centers; thus the experimental rockets would not be likely to cause any damage to life or property when they returned to earth. Since there were few people native to the locality, few had had to be displaced. The constancy of the climate was a big factor also, for bad weather would hinder test flights and so delay progress.

Only one road led into the bowl, and for the past three days it had been jammed with traffic. And on this thirtieth day of June the cars were lined as far as one could see. The rim of the bowl was black with spectators, some of whom had been camping for days, so great was their curiosity and eagerness to have a part, no matter how small, in the launching of this immense rocket. The crowd was a motley array of sun umbrellas, tents, blankets, and anything else that might serve as a shield against the blazing sun.

The opinions of the people were mixed. Some were doubters, like the elderly, well-dressed man who had come in during the night. He was talking with a group of onlookers.

"If they'd worry a little less about what's up there," he said as he pointed to the sky, "and pay more attention to what's right here—" he pointed repeatedly at the parched sand on which they were standing—"we'd all be better off."

A young fellow in the crowd grunted loudly. "Humph," he said, "you don't have to worry about that, pop. They'll never get there anyway. Soon as the rocket gets away from the earth, it'll bust up. Pieces of it will be spread all over the place."

"What do you mean?" a voice from the back of the group asked. "They got to the moon didn't they?"

The young fellow agreed. "Yeah, they got to the moon. But getting to Mars is a lot harder. They'll never make it. You just wait and see."

There were many who agreed with these ideas. But there were others, by far the majority, who believed that the rocket would reach the red planet.

"They're going to make great discoveries," they said. "Who knows, maybe they'll find the roots of life so we can live a thousand years or more."

"A thousand years!" some exclaimed. "Who'd ever want to live that long. Give me my three score and ten, and make them good ones and I'll be happy."

There was not much that the spectators could see besides the rocket, which was mounted upright, its nose pointing to the zenith, and an occasional movement here and there. They relaxed like an empty balloon and filled the long hours of waiting with speculative talk.

Suddenly the crowd perked up as they sighted a jeep moving rapidly over a roadway of linked steel sections from the center of the bowl toward the cluster of low buildings which was the supply depot.

A stout spectator wearing a white pith helmet and huge polaroid goggles removed his cigar from his mouth and stared at the jeep. More to himself than to those around him, he said, "Man, look at that jeep go. The bird driving that don't believe in dust settling on him."

It was true that Jack Strong didn't believe in poking along. The jeep driver was the youngest member of the three-man crew of the rocket ship. He was eighteen years old and just entering college when he was selected for this great adventure.

In high school he had not been spectacular. He was too small for the varsity teams; and, although he held many lesser offices, he never became the president of any organization. But he was active and likable, and everyone knew Jack Strong was around. Although he was about average in his subjects (except Latin, which he flunked), he was outstanding in science. Ever since his freshman year, he had had an average of ninety-five in science.

Now Jack was driving fast, knowing that this was one place he could speed with safety, for the roadway was smooth and straight, and his was the only vehicle on it. Whenever he went to the supply depot, his foot was heavy on the gas pedal.

"Now who'd be comin' high-tailin' it like that," said Tex, a tall, slightly bowlegged cowpuncher who was leaning against a steel fence pole near the entrance to the depot. "As if I don't know." He took a straw from his mouth and spat into the sand. "Only Jack Strong would be loopin' like that. Young sprout can't seem to go fast enough."

Tex was a native of the region who had come riding in one day to find out what was going on when he saw the buildings going up. The supply engineer liked him at once and convinced Tex that he should work at the depot. Tex had been there ever since.

The supply depot was a series of four large warehouses, two on each side of the wide steel roadway that ran between them. In the center of the roadway was a booth that housed switches and controls. These regulated the opening and closing of each warehouse, and also fired the security guns. The guns were fired automatically at anyone who was not cleared by the main office and who moved within the radar screen around each building. Fifty feet from each structure a heavy radar barrier was set up. When anyone moved through this, a loudspeaker warned, "Do not go ahead. Move away from this building. An automatic rifle is aimed at you and will fire in thirty seconds.'" The weirdness of hearing a sound when there was no human in sight with whom an intruder might argue was baffling. When a stranger heard the warning, he lost no time in getting away from the danger zone.

Jack pulled up at the outer gate, squealing the tires to a stop.

"Hi, Tex," he shouted as he waved, "I thought I'd run over and pay you a visit."

"Hello, young feller," said Tex as he rolled toward the jeep. "They's more to yore comin' than a visit. Ever'body that comes here is wantin' somethin'."

Tex blinked his small blue eyes that were wrinkled and faded by many years of desert sun. He pointed an accusing finger at Jack.

"And another thing, young feller. You better take it easy. No need to go speedin' around the way you do. First thing you know you'll smash yerself up."

"I wasn't speeding, Tex."

Jack saw the frown of disbelief on Tex's face. "Well not much anyway. We'll be going a lot faster than that this afternoon when the rocket takes off."

"Humph," grunted Tex as he stepped into the jeep and sprawled in the seat beside Jack. "There ain't no sense in it. We got enough troubles right here, without goin' off into the sky and findin' more."

Jack had learned that nothing would convince Tex of the value of the journey into space so he made no comment. He put the jeep into gear and started up so fast that Tex was thrown hard against the back of the seat, and his ten-gallon hat slipped to the back of his head.

After the jeep had gained speed and Tex had replaced his hat, he spoke. "What you after this time, young feller? I knowed soon's I saw you comin' you was wantin' somethin'."

"As a matter of fact there is something, Tex." Tex nodded his head knowingly. "This is the last trip I'll be making over here for some time. I'm after the plutonium. That's the last cargo to go aboard."

"What's that?" asked Tex as he held to the brim of his hat. "I've got iron and steel, nuts and bolts, tools and gasoline, and jest about ever'thin' else. But no plutarium, or whatever you call it."

Tex was pulling Jack's leg as he often did, for no one in the '80's was ignorant of this wonder metal.

"It's plutonium," said Jack, enunciating each syllable carefully. "And I know you have it here. It's in those red and white cases that came the other day."

"Oh, them things," said Tex. "I was wonderin' what they was. Pull over to the security office. Don't want to be blown to pieces by the automatic guns."

A few minutes later Jack pulled up the jeep before the first warehouse. "If it's the bright red and white things you're after, we'll find 'em here," said Tex as he unwound from the jeep. When he stood up, he towered above the thing as a child towers above a toy wagon.

"Plutonium," he mumbled to himself as he slouched

toward the door. "Plutonium and rockets that fly into the sky to who knows where. Nothin' but foolishness."

He unclipped a key ring that he wore fastened to his belt and inserted a key in a small box next to the door as he mumbled to himself.

A red light above the box blinked on and off. The crackle of a loudspeaker could be heard, and then a voice boomed, "Warehouse one—check in."

Tex spoke into the box which contained a sensitive microphone, "Tex, checkin' fer clearance."

The loudspeaker commanded, "Give the password."

"Igloo," said Tex. And as he turned toward Jack, he mumbled, "Lot o' foolishness."

This was an additional precaution. The doors could be opened only by the security booth, and only after a special key had been inserted in the loudspeaker box. The doors now slid back and Tex entered the building. Both walls were lined with every conceivable type of equipment: lumber, nails, wire, tools, fencing, oil, grease, hardware, sheet metal, steel beams. The center was clear so that trucks could move the length of the building.

Tex beckoned to Jack to drive in.

"Move on down a ways," drawled Tex. He seemed to lope beside the jeep that was idling along.

"Here they are," he said as he laid a hand on the second of the three cases. "There's yore plutonium."

"Right you are, Tex. That's the stuff all right. You can see those bright cases a mile away. It's the fuel for the ship."

The cases were metal cubes, two feet in each dimension. They were painted with alternate stripes of bright red and white, the code color for plutonium.

"You mean they's enough here to make that big rocket go as fer as yore wantin' it to go?"

"There sure is, Tex. And the cubes are not all plutonium, either. Most of the case is shielding. The plutonium in each one isn't much bigger than a brick."

"Well, I'll be doggoned," said Tex as he hefted a case. "They're sure heavy enough though. Have to get the hoist, I reckon."

The hoist was a four-wheeled loading device that ran on storage batteries. Tex returned on it, scooped up the cases, and set them down in the rear of the jeep.

"Thanks," said Jack. "I'll do the same for you some day. Coming over to see us off, aren't you?"

"Dunno yet. Mebbe I will if I have the time."

From Tex, who hated to commit himself, this meant he was accepting the invitation with enthusiasm.

"Good," said Jack as he started the engine. "I'll be looking for you."

"You take it easy now, young feller. You don't have to break a record gettin' back there. They'll wait fer you."

"Okay, Tex, I promise."

And there wasn't any racing on the way back. Tex knew that Jack would drive slowly, for he had made a promise to. And Tex had often remarked, "I sure like that young fellow over at the rocket. When he says he'll do a thing, it's good as done. Yessir, with him a promise is a promise and no foolin'."

Jack drove along slowly, gazing ahead over the rolling dunes. His thoughts chased one another.

The people along the rim of the bowl watched the jeep closely.

"The jeep's not going so fast now," said the stout spectator as he lowered a match from a freshly lit cigar. "He's just poking along."

"Maybe he's got something on back that'll blow up if it jounces," said a shallow-chested stranger alongside him. "He's going straight for the rocket, though. It can't be too dangerous."

The eyes of the odd-looking pair, and the eyes of the entire crowd, followed the jeep to the rocket, which dominated the bowl and the buildings in it. The rocket was a great silver bullet with a needle nose, which rose out of the desert sands much as a lone candle appears to rise out of the birthday cake it decorates. The mellow silver of the rocket caught the morning sunlight and glowed like a polished opal. The outer jacket was made of titanium, a metal that reflected sunlight and thus made temperature control easier. But the main reason for using this metal was its great strength. It was considerably stronger than steel, but it weighed much less. The development of this metal was what made possible the building of the rocket, for great strength was essential, but weight had to be kept low. Before titanium was introduced, steel was the only metal that had the required strength; and its weight was prohibitively high.

Jack's eyes rested on the rocket. It was one hundred feet over all, from the tip of its shiny nose to the hindmost stabilizing fins, and sixteen feet in outside diameter at the widest point.

"*Lodestar* is a good name for her," thought Jack. "It fits her just right."

The rocket was smooth and tapering, except for the three stabilizing fins that projected from it along the lower third of its length. These vanes were planned to keep the ship from wobbling during the initial acceleration, as well as during the landing on Mars. The stern of the ship was open. A great blast of superheated gases would be expelled through this opening, forcing the ship ahead. And the crew entered their compartment through this opening.

The sun was beating down upon Jack so he went a little faster to get out of the relentless heat. When he pulled up before the *Lodestar*, Mr. Warick was waiting for him.

Donald Warick was a friendly, smiling person. He was

unmarried and had no relatives dependent upon him. This accounted in part for his daring, for he had no one to think about but himself. He had lost both his parents in a tragic airplane crash when he was very young, and he had spent most of his early life in a children's home. As a child, he was always tinkering with clocks, cars, and any other machinery that he could find. He had an inborn mechanical aptitude. Because of this and also because of his outstanding work in the Boy Scouts of America, he was selected as a junior mechanic on a uranium hunting expedition to the Antarctic region. The men on this expedition encouraged him to use his mechanical abilities more widely. They inspired him to go to college and become an engineer. He saw that he needed book learning to round out his practical experience and ability. After long years of struggle he earned his way through college and graduated with honors.

Like many people who have no relatives close to them and who have fought hard for their success, Mr. Warick was self-centered. He was particular, almost finicky, about his appearance—and one of his passions was ties; he liked them bright and different. When he saw a new design, he couldn't resist buying it. He was a frugal person in other matters, but about ties he was extravagant. His cocky confidence was balanced by a ready humor. It was his uncanny mechanical ability, however, that brought him the coveted position of chief engineer and mechanic of the *Lodestar*.

Mr. Warick strode to the jeep and leaned over the brightly striped cases that Jack had brought, reading the labels that were printed on them.

"What's new with Tex?" he asked.

"Not a thing," answered Jack. "He's still growling about this whole deal. Thinks it's a lot of nonsense."

Mr. Warick grinned understandingly at Jack. "Enough of that, let's see to these cases."

Two workmen had come over to the jeep to help with the unloading. "Just help us get these on the ground," said Mr. Warick. "Jack and I will get the stuff aboard." Don usually had complete confidence in the work of others, for all the workers were carefully selected; but the installation of the plutonium was a job he entrusted to no one but himself.

He and Jack removed the striped outer cases with great care. Plain wooden boxes were inside these. Another wooden box, surrounded by exploded mica, which served as an insulator and shock absorber, was inside this. They removed these cases and opened them to disclose more of this same mica insulator and absorber.

Jack had never seen a plutonium shipment before. As he dug into the mica he discovered a square box covered with red and white stripes that was even brighter than the red used on the outer covering. This was a glow paint that almost screamed danger.

"What's this?" asked Jack. "I never saw anything so red in my life."

"It's the bimag case, Jack. Don't try to remove it. We don't take that off until we're ready to slip the plutonium into position."

Bimag was a coined word composed of the *b* from beryllium, the *i* from iron, and the *mag* from magnesium. These three metals were alloyed to make a highly efficient radiation reflector, and plutonium was always placed inside a case made of this metal until it was put into a reactor. In the 1950's, when atomic research was in its infancy, lead had to be used as a barrier. This was heavy and cumbersome, and it was also relatively scarce. Bimag was a decisive step forward from lead.

"Here's the last of them," said Mr. Warick as he uncovered the third cube. "Let's set them in place."

He picked up two of the cubes, and Jack carried the third. The cubes were only ten inches square and were therefore easy to handle, although they were very heavy. The men entered the tail of the ship. Temporary electric lights that would soon be removed lighted their way as they moved upward toward the very heart of the ship —the atomic reactor. It was truly the heart, for it provided all the energy to drive the rocket, as well as the power needed to light the ship, cook food, heat the crew compartment, and operate the multitude of controls.

The core of the reactor was extremely small, only two feet wide, two feet deep, and three feet long. Its total weight was about eight hundred pounds, including the shielding. The fuel alone in the old-fashioned rockets in use after the second world war weighed as much as twenty thousand pounds: five tons of alcohol and five tons of liquid oxygen.

The operation of the reactor was similar to that of the first atomic piles that were built during the research in the 1940's that was to lead to the atomic bomb. This reactor was much more efficient than those early ones, however, and it did not require as heavy insulation. But cadmium was still used as a moderator to speed up or slow down the reaction.

Mr. Warick slid back a panel that covered the reactor. Jack and he were on their knees, peering into the maze of tubes that wound through it. The bimag cubes were alongside them.

"Well, here goes," said Mr. Warick as he reached for one of the brightly striped cubes. "This is the final warm-up."

He reached into the cube with long forceps and re-moved a solid chunk of grayish-black metal, not much larger than a couple of packs of cigarettes. This was a highly radioactive isotope of plutonium. He nonchalantly slipped it into a small compartment in the reactor.

"That's all there is to it," he said as he slid back the panel. "Now let's go into the crew compartment and we'll stow these other cubes."

Climbing into the crew compartment was like stepping inside a rubber ball. They stepped into soft, responsive foam rubber, and on all sides were walls of the same material. Behind this shock-absorbing material there were countless cabinets and storage bins containing all manner of elaborate equipment; such as concentrated foods, seeds, drugs, tools, and space suits. Each piece of apparatus was placed in its compartment to prevent breakage and to make location easier later on as it was required. Every inch of space was utilized.

Overhead was the instrument panel, behind a lattice-work of resilient, semielastic bands. In flight the panel would be the forward end of the crew compartment; but now, because the ship was standing on its tail, it was above them. The panel was so large that it covered the entire ceiling.

On the instrument board there were controls which regulated the oxygen supply in the compartment. These were arranged so that they kept the supply at a normal concentration automatically. If the reserves were dangerously low, the levers could be set at minimum, which would give the crew just enough oxygen to sustain life. The men had been trained to fly for long periods of time at this low level, so that if they had to resort to it they would be able to do so without fainting.

There were instruments of all types and sizes: some were the diameter of a basketball and others were no larger than a pocket watch. The background of the panel was dull black. Each instrument was painted with fluorescent paint, and was illuminated by ultraviolet beams that caused them to glow softly. There were clocks set to keep civil time as well as star time. There were radiation gauges, temperature gauges and regulators, voltmeters and ammeters, rate of climb indicators, and acceleration dials. A large part of the panel was devoted to the automatic pilot devices, and to the long-range radar installation, including the oscilloscope.

Mr. Warick folded back one of the rubber panels along the bulkhead, opened a cabinet, and placed the bimag cubes inside it. The cubes were held securely by clamps that were covered with heavy thicknesses of rubber to prevent shock. He peered up at the instrument panel, moving his head to one side to look at a temperature dial and the radiation indicator.

"See there, Jack," he said as he squinted through the bands, "she's creeping up already."

The safety bands looked like cotton but they were

woven of a plastic and silk mixture that made them stronger than steel and much more pliable. They made seeing rather difficult; but it was essential that they be placed in front of the panel as a precaution against breakage. They would also protect the crew from crashing into the panel if their belts should break.

Jack craned his neck from side to side to get a view. "Sure doesn't take long, does it? Look at that radiation dial! It's jumping back and forth like a clock pendulum." The action was always erratic when a plutonium breakdown started, but even as Jack spoke the dial steadied at a mark halfway to maximum, indicating that the reactor was warming up and functioning properly.

The crew compartment was dominated by three elaborate seats, one for each member of the crew. The seats were the bucket type. They were mounted so that they remained level no matter at what angle the ship was tilted. This was done by fastening the seat above the center of gravity to a horizontal bar, around which the seat was free to move. This bar was set into a large vertical metal ring about four feet in diameter. The bar was free to move around the circle; thus it made a movable diameter. The seats themselves were heavily padded with foam rubber that was covered with a durable, leatherlike plastic. In addition to the foam rubber, there were air cushions to reduce the take-off and landing shock. Each seat had numerous straps hanging from it. These were fastened about the men before the take-off. The seats moved on friction bearings which held the seats steady at all times.

"It looks as if everything's in order here, Jack," said Mr. Warick as he moved toward the escape door. "Let's go out and check with the boss."

"Right you are, Mr. Warick. Go ahead down and I'll follow."

As they neared the exhaust tubes Mr. Warick laughed slightly and said, "I wouldn't want to be near these a few hours from now."

"Golly, neither would I," said Jack as he climbed down the ladder. "We'd be changed to gas before we knew what had happened."

The exhaust tubes were made of a highly heat-resistant iron alloy, and were lined with a claylike material made from diatomaceous earth. This is a type of limestone that was formed from the skeletons of diatoms, small animals of the sea. This made an effective heat insulator.

As Jack and Mr. Warick emerged from the rocket, the heat of the mid-morning sun struck them like a blow-torch.

"Wow," said Jack. "I'll bet this is the hottest day yet. I'll never get used to this heat."

"You won't have to, Jack. In a few more hours you can kiss this old oven good-by."

Jack looked toward the administration building. A station wagon had just pulled up.

"Hey," he shouted, "maybe that's my folks over there. Come on over and see."

The two of them started to trot, but the heat quickly slowed them down to a walk. Jack hugged his mother and kissed her on the cheek. "Gosh, Mom, I'm sure glad to see you," he said as he held her by the shoulders at arm's length.

She was smiling proudly. "There's your father," she said, "don't be forgetting him."

Jack and his father shook hands warmly and firmly. It was a handshake that said all those things that men feel and want to say to each other, but seldom do.

Mr. Warick greeted Jack's parents, then excused himself, saying, "Why don't you show your mother and dad around the ship. While you're busy, I'll report to Dr. Shallot."

Jack took his parents to the security booth where they were photographed and interrogated. In a few minutes they were given clearance, and they walked together toward the *Lodestar*.

"It certainly is impressive," said Jack's father. "We thought, in your letters, that you were exaggerating about the ship; but she certainly is a beautiful thing. This is the smoothest surface I've ever seen."

"It sure is," said Jack, "for it's the smoothest that any surface as large as this has ever been made, Dad. The slightest roughness would set up so much friction and heat that the cooling coils wouldn't be able to take it away fast enough."

His mother had her hand in the crook of Jack's arm. "Who's going to do the cooking, Jack?"

"We'll all take turns, Mom."

"Take turns," she exclaimed, "that'll be some cooking. What will you eat?"

"It won't be very good, I'm afraid. But it will be nourishing," he added quickly. "We've made sure of it. Everything has been tested over and over again. Of course almost everything is either dehydrated or condensed; but it'll keep us going."

"Humph," she grumbled, "dehydrated and condensed. You'll be getting thin on that sort of food." She pushed a wicker basket with a cover on it into his hands. "Here's something you'll like, and it's not dried or condensed. It's just plain food."

"But, Mom," Jack objected without thinking. "I can't take it. There's no room for anything."

"Nonsense, there's always room for a little basket like that."

She didn't realize that the weight of the *Lodestar* had been reckoned to the last ounce.

"Better take it," said his father. "She prepared it specially."

"Okay, Mom," he said, "and thanks a lot. I can guess what's in it."

Jack knew that his mother would have felt bad had he not taken it. But he knew also that he couldn't take it aboard ship, so he planned to turn it over to the ground crew.

After being passed on by the triple guards around the ship, Jack helped his parents into the *Lodestar*.

As they were climbing the temporary ladder, his father asked, "How fast do you expect to go?"

"We don't know for sure, but we hope it will be around 25,000 miles an hour. We have to go at least that fast to hit our target at the spot we plan."

"That's what the papers said, but we really couldn't believe it," said his father incredulously. "Why, why it's like—" And not knowing what it was like, he added, "It's more than I can begin to understand. And suppose you do go that fast. How will you ever slow down again?"

"That part will be easy. There are jets in the nose of the ship that force the ship backward. When we want to slow down, these jets will be turned on. The first blast of heat will melt off the alloy that covers the tubes flush with the skin of the ship. Then the forward blasts will cut down our velocity."

They were now in the crew compartment, and Jack explained the instrument panel to his father; then he showed him how the storage cabinets were arranged behind the foam-rubber lining. He set his mother in his own seat and strapped her in loosely while explaining the instrument panel.

"See that big greenish circle up there?" he asked. "That shows a picture of everything outside that's around us. It works sort of like television. The tube's just the same as the one in our set back home.

"And see that block of dials on the right?" he continued. "They tell us the temperature all over the ship. One says how warm it is in the power plant, another gives the temperature at the nose of the ship, the sides of it and the jet tube."

"I declare," said his mother as she gazed at the bewildering array of dials, levers, and controls, "I don't see how you can make head or tail of them."

She was glad to leave the ship for she felt pressed in by the limited space. She said nothing of this to Jack, however. She was fingering a small square of cloth that was sewed securely. "Son," she said as she handed the packet to Jack, "I want you to take this with you. It's a bit of earth from your own back yard. When you get to Mars, away off there, I want you to sprinkle it on the ground. It'll be a little spot of us in the universe."

Jack was pleased. "What a wonderful idea, Mother." He brushed her cheek with his lips. "Good old Mom, you always think up something nice and different."

Jack noticed a flurry of dust on the ridge where the road slid down into the bowl.

"Wow!" he cried, "here comes the send-off committee. I'll have to hurry."

He bustled his parents to the administration building and seated them comfortably.

"Wait here," he said, "and I'll be back in a jiffy. I have to get into my uniform."

Several minutes later Jack reappeared in an immaculate one-piece tan coverall made of the finest grade of virgin wool gabardine. Extensive tests were made with all kinds of synthetic fabrics, but virgin wool surpassed all others as a clothing fabric. A soft, visored cap of the same material was in his hand.

"Well," he said, "how do I look?"

Tears came to his mother's eyes. "Wonderful," she said huskily as she touched the tip of her handkerchief to her eyes, "just wonderful."

Jack ignored the tears, for he knew his mother would be embarrassed if he commented on them. "Come on," he said as he helped his mother from her chair, "let's look up Dr. Shallot and Mr. Warick. We'll all go to the ceremonies together."

Because they were too far away, the spectators could not see the send-off ceremonies that were being held near the base of the rocket. However, many of them had pocket radios and could pick up the broadcast version. There was no brass band or parade, but only a sincere farewell given to the crew by their associates, relatives, and a few important government officials.

A spectator with field glasses accounted to those around him what was taking place. "Looks like they're finished talking," he said. "Everybody's getting into the cars and driving off. Yep, there's only three of them left. Must be the crew, I guess."

The visitors and technicians were driven to low concrete structures that had been built toward the edge of the bowl. The cars entered the buildings through thick concrete walls reinforced with steel matting. These buildings were strong enough to protect the occupants from debris should the rocket explode. The flat roof of the structure was dotted with small peep windows of heavy heat- and shock-resistant glass, through which the occupants could watch the ship.

As the cars disappeared within the concrete buildings, a small helicopter took off and circled upward. It moved toward the rim of the bowl, hovering there while instructions were given to the crowd over a loudspeaker. "Attention, attention, attention," it boomed forth in a deep, commanding tone. "All spectators are warned to follow these instructions exactly. When you hear the siren and see the red lights blinking, close your eyes. Lie flat on your stomach with your head away from the bowl. Remove all dark clothing, or cover it with something white." Actually no one in dark clothing had been allowed within the outer gate, so this part of the warning was unnecessary.

The helicopter moved slowly around the bowl, blaring out the same message over and over again.

The stout spectator whose cigar had long been out, but who chewed on it nevertheless, said to his companion, "Be kinda bad if a fellow had on a dark blue suit. He'd have to peel down to his shorts."

"He might better do that," said a person near by, "than get burned. When that rocket takes off it's going to be plenty warm around here, and black things absorb the heat. If you're in dark clothes, you'll get burned. White ones, you're okay."

The helicopter settled down on the landing strip, shut off its rotors and was pulled inside the hangar. The entire bowl was encased in a great quiet which everyone felt a need to keep. All talking was done in whispers. The hush was heavy, like the stillness of a football crowd during a crucial play. This was not a restful quiet, but one of tension and excitement, a quiet where the beating of a heart reverberates in the ears like the pounding of a sledge hammer.

Jack Strong could feel the quiet tension as he, Mr. Warick, and Dr. Shallot, the leader of the mission, stood before the *Lodestar*, poised for flight. The ship was held erect by a tripod cradle of steel girders that extended forty feet above the ground. While the *Lodestar* was being built, scaffolds had ridden up and down the uprights which extended above the cradle, but these were now removed.

Auxiliary rockets were to be used for the take-off instead of the nuclear jet, for the jet would spray the countryside for miles around with deadly radioactive gases. The rockets were mounted on a ring that pushed against the fattest part of the ship. When the rockets were spent, the ring and rocket assemblies would drop to the earth,

for they would be of no further use and would only break
the smooth flow of air over the ship.

Dr. Shallot rubbed his right temple, which he did
whenever he was engrossed. For so many years he had
done this that his right temple was almost bald. "They
certainly treated us nicely, didn't they?" he said.

"They certainly did," agreed Mr. Warick. Then he
added jokingly, "I never knew anyone cared that much
about me. Maybe they think they can afford to be nice
'cause they won't be seeing us for a while."

"Then we'd better get going before they change their
minds," said Jack. And he added seriously, "But it gives
you a warm feeling to know so many people are believing
in you; maybe even more than you believe in yourself."

"It does, Jack. We have a responsibility to those people
out there."

As he spoke, Dr. Shallot surveyed the bowl. Four heavy
army trucks with cantilever towers had driven within a
thousand feet of the rocket and had raised their towers
on which automatic cameras were mounted. Green lights
shone from each of the towers, indicating that the cameras
were rolling, and that the cameramen had taken cover.
A large green flag flapped lazily in the breeze above the
concrete structure that housed the visitors, showing that
all were in readiness there. Dr. Shallot turned to the men
and added, "It looks as if everything's under control."

"Switch on your radio, Jack," he said, "and we'll see if we can get clearance."

Jack snapped the switch of his small two-way pocket radio and handed it to Dr. Shallot.

"Hello, tower. This is *Lodestar* calling."

There was a crackle followed by the voice of the dispatcher. "Hello, *Lodestar,* we hear you. Come in."

As he listened, Jack's eyes wandered over his surroundings. The sun was beating down from a position almost directly overhead, making shadows small and sharp. No individuals could be distinguished from where he stood but he could see the mass of spectators swelling the rim of the bowl. His eyes ran slowly up the body of the ship which towered above him, and beyond that to the blue, cloudless sky that was their uncharted road to Mars. His stomach felt heavy and large enough to fill his whole body.

"Crew ready to enter ship," said the doctor crisply. "Take-off fifteen minutes after last man enters. Please give clearance."

"All clear, *Lodestar*. You may proceed." The harsh official tone of the dispatcher was dropped and replaced with a cordial one. "And good luck to all of you, Doctor."

Dr. Shallot acknowledged the good wishes and switched off the radio, for he disliked elaborate ceremony. With a last quick look all around the bowl he said, "Well, gentlemen, this is it. There go our last ties to mother earth. From now on we three are on our own completely."

They stepped to the base of the ship, first Dr. Shallot, then Mr. Warick, and finally Jack. When they reached the gaping jet tube, the leader spoke to Jack. "You're the youngest, Jack. We'll give you the honor of entering first."

Jack gulped, "Yes, sir." He looked about him and then swung himself into the bowels of the rocket. The men could go straight through the power plant and into the crew compartment without using the air lock, a device for adjusting to pressure changes which would be needed when they disembarked. By entering through the jet tube a crew door was eliminated, thus the sleekness of the ship was unbroken. Jack climbed through the exhaust tube, past the reactor whose warmth he could feel, and into the crew compartment. Mr. Warick followed immediately behind Jack, and Dr. Shallot was the last to enter.

The ship had no openings to the outside except one small peep sight, no larger than a twenty-five-cent piece. But even though it was small, the sight contained wide angle lenses that provided a broad field of vision. The crew was not aware of the lack of openings, for the interior was diffused with an illumination like daylight that was produced by fluorescent tubes activated by high-frequency signals.

When the doctor entered the crew compartment he closed and fastened securely the double titanium doors. There was no indecision about what was to do done, for each man had learned through months of training the steps that were to be followed. They put on acceleration suits over their tan coveralls and replaced their soft visored caps with tight-fitting crash helmets. The acceleration suits were corsets that fit very tightly about the stomach and lower back as well as the groin. They were designed to diminish the flow of blood from the head and thus decrease the aftereffects of the inevitable blackout.

Jack checked the closure of the doors through which they had entered, as this was one of his responsibilities, and then hampered by the corset, he struggled stiffly to his seat. Since the rocket was vertical, the seats were overhead and could be entered only by climbing the rope ladders that were suspended from them. Dr. Shallot sat in his chair which in flight would be directly in the center of the main control panel. Mr. Warick sat in his chair which was to the left of Dr. Shallot and a foot or so behind him, and Jack sat on Dr. Shallot's right.

All three of them were very tense, and they made no pretense at conversation. Each one wanted to be alone with his thoughts and his prayers. The three of them gazed over their heads through the fabric webbing at the instrument panel which was aglow with blinkers of various colors. The radiation dial which showed the activity in the nuclear reactor was holding at a steady medium.

Dr. Shallot peered closely at the dials and checked all

the lights. He ordered them to strap down. This meant they were to fasten heavy belts around their chests and stomachs to hold them in their seats. Then each one placed a heavy band around his head to which a spring was attached. This kept their heads from being bent too far forward. The doctor turned stiffly to Mr. Warick.

"Ready, Don?" he asked in a tone much deeper and huskier than usual.

Don answered crisply, "Ready, sir. Let her go."

"Ready, Jack?" asked the doctor.

"Ready, sir," Jack answered, although later on he couldn't remember having said anything at all.

The doctor reached overhead and pushed the activator button. Nothing happened that could be seen; but in the power plant a mechanism was sliding the cadmium control rods out of the nuclear reactor and was allowing the heat to build up so the nuclear jet could take over after the auxiliary rockets were exhausted.

The men were speechless and motionless. They gazed at the radiation dial and watched it creep slowly but steadily toward maximum. They watched the dial that registered the temperature of the jet tube creep to a thousand, fifteen hundred, two thousand, twenty-five hundred degrees. No one was afraid. At least their teeth were not chattering nor were their bodies covered with goose pimples; but they were apprehensive, for no one knew what would happen next. They were the test pilots, the guinea pigs who would tell the world whether or not a rocket could reach another planet.

When the temperature dial moved up to three thousand degrees, the doctor ordered in a voice that was stern and compelling, "Fold up."

This was the signal for Jack and Don to bundle themselves into balls within their restraining belts. They folded their knees against their chests and placed their heads on their knees. A wide belt encircled their knees and held them in this position. Numerous tests had been made to find the best flight position, and this was the most effective. In experiments with sheep and monkeys no position had been found that prevented the loss of blood from the head and the resultant blackouts; but it was discovered that the doubled-up posture caused the least damage to the small blood vessels that heretofore were permanently injured if the test animals were held in normal positions.

When Mr. Warick and Jack were folded up, Dr. Shallot said reverently, "May God be with us."

As he spoke he kicked the acceleration lever with a decisive motion, then folded up quickly within his restraining belt. For a few moments that seemed like an eternity, nothing happened. And then they heard a deep rumble that grew louder and louder until it almost deafened them, even though heavy helmets covered their ears. Their stomachs pushed harder and harder against their backs. They felt heavier and heavier, so heavy that they could not move the smallest part of their bodies. They felt sick, scared, bewildered, weak, giddy, faint. The doctor fainted and was followed seconds later by Don and then Jack. Their inert bodies were held in position by the numerous straps and belts that had been fastened securely about them.

"What did I tell you?" said the young skeptic who had predicted that the rocket wouldn't reach Mars. "They can't even get the thing off the ground." He said this after the crew had been in the ship for ten minutes, and exhaust gases were already visible from the idling jets as they preheated the auxiliary rocket tubes.

The fat man said, "They're not ready yet. Takes some time to warm up, you know. They'll get off all right. Twelve o'clock is when they're supposed to go, and they won't go any sooner than that. Just hold your horses; it won't be long because it's almost twelve now."

And it was not long. In a few minutes the first notes of a siren could be heard. It wailed louder and louder, and batteries of red flood lights blinked on and off, moving through a complete circle so that all could see. The crowd, moving as a single person, prostrated themselves on the hot sand and covered their eyes. They could see no more, but their ears were filled with a deafening roar that covered up the wailing sirens, overpowering them as though they never existed.

The observers in the concrete structures looked through the small windows. They saw the exhaust gases build up in thickness and force until the air was filled with hot, blistering sand particles picked up by the gases, filling the bowl like a low hanging cloud. They saw a brilliant white ball of fire and flame, and immediately above it they could see the hazy outlines of the rocket. It was poised in mid-air, as if resting on the ball of fire. This was perhaps only an illusion, for the next moment the ship was moving away from them at an unbelievable rate of speed. Nothing but a trailing tail of fire was visible.

When the fat man threw himself down on the sand, he counted slowly to himself, "One, two, three, four, five." When he reached five he could not hear the siren, and the explosion was only an echo that had settled down to a receding roar, so he turned over on his back and gazed at the sky. He shook the man next to him roughly. "Look," he shouted loudly, "hurry. It's gone. You can't even see the thing."

And you couldn't. The observers could see nothing but a dull red glow that was the hot gases expanding through the jet tube. In a few seconds the *Lodestar* had dropped her earthly ties and had become a traveler through the endless reaches of space.

3. THE CREW CHIEF

THE *LODESTAR* was man's first attempt to reach
another planet, but it was not his first venture into space.
Research and experimental flights had been started some
fifty years before, during and immediately after the
second world war. So called V-2 rockets had reached over
a hundred miles above the earth. These used various
chemical fuels, among which were liquid oxygen, alcohol,
hydrogen peroxide, and potassium permanganate. Because of the tremendous amount of fuel required, the
weight of which was often three times that of the rocket
itself, these V-2 rockets could not attain a great enough
acceleration to reach higher altitudes. After some years
of experimentation a step rocket was made. This was
actually two rockets, one of which started its flight when
the first had reached its summit and became disengaged.
The second one reached an altitude of 250 miles. This
was virtually outside the earth's atmosphere.

But 250 miles was the limit to which a rocket, even the step variety, could reach so long as it was dependent upon chemical fuel. And such a rocket could not approach the seven-miles-a-second speed necessary to escape from the gravitational pull of the earth. The advent of atomic energy held a new promise, but it was not until the last decade that scientists had found a way of taming the energy of a nuclear pile and of using it to gasify water, superheat it, and thus produce a super fuel that was capable of exerting a powerful force over a period of hours, rather than seconds, or at the most minutes. Minutes, heretofore, were the limit of force one could get from chemical fuels.

After unmanned rockets and probes had been crashed into the moon and instruments had been soft-landed, technicians were convinced that a man-carrying rocket could reach the moon, land, take off, and return to the earth. Twenty years before, astronauts had made several journeys to the moon and had carried off the missions with great success.

They had brought back a vast amount of information about the moon, much of which supported the best thought-out theories of the day. They found, for example, that the moon is a barren waste covered with several inches, and in some cases several feet, of volcanic ash or powdered pumice. It was proved that there is no water at all on the moon, that the temperatures are extreme, as high as 250 degrees Fahrenheit in the daytime and as low as 150 degrees below zero at night. The cliffs are abrupt, rising several hundred feet straight into the air, and they are jagged, sharp, forbidding, and unscalable. The bedrock of the moon is granitic, and whatever minerals are found there are deeply encased and therefore difficult to get.

In addition to the knowledge of the moon that was obtained, much valuable data was produced which would make future trips into space more feasible. Scientists learned how necessary it was to devise a method for avoiding or counteracting the effect of meteoric collisions, one of the most disastrous obstacles to success. They were given data that helped them design safer, more stable seats. And they were given facts about take-off conditions from a place where the air is less dense than that on earth and where the gravitational pull is less. Rocket scientists were delighted with the details of space flying that were learned, for they pointed the way toward the realization of interplanetary travel.

Even though much information was garnered by this expedition, there were many questions that were still unanswered, questions that had been irking mankind for generations, and about which there was much speculation. Is there life on any of the other heavenly bodies in

our solar system and, for that matter, is there life anywhere else in the entire universe? And if there is life, is
it vegetable or animal? If it should be animal does that
life take the form of humans as we know them, or is there
a form of higher animal life that cannot be comprehended
by man? Are there creatures existing on other planets who
have learned the mysteries of the mind and are therefore
superior to man? Such were some of the questions that
remained unanswered and for which Dr. Shallot and his
friends hoped to find explanations.

But questions dealing with the origins of life, and the
possibility of life existing on other planets, were super-
seded by other, more pressing, considerations. Many astronomers believed that Mars was a dying planet, a planet
that had reached its peak some milleniums ago and was
becoming or had become lifeless and extinct. And they
believed strongly that the earth was destined to go
through this same series of events, snuffing out all life and
becoming a cold wasteland. They believed that the crew
could find how the Martians fared during the dying-out
period, and what was more vital, what had caused the
breakdown of the planet. By knowing this the people on
earth could prepare for the inevitable, or they could perhaps stave off the collapse so that the planet and its civilization would survive.

In addition to finding solutions to these perplexing
problems, there were assignments that the expedition to

Mars had to carry out for various government agencies. The agricultural offices wanted a study made of the plant life, and samples of it brought back. If there were plants that bore seeds, they wanted some of these seeds. And if the plant life were composed of ferns and molds, they wanted spores of these so they could attempt to grow them on earth. The geologic office wanted a detailed study made of the terrain, and of the minerals making up the crust as well as the sublayer of the planet. These samples were to be carefully labeled and catalogued so that accurate models of the planet could be constructed. The office of defense wanted all sorts of data, such as samples of the atmosphere, available minerals of strategic value, and the estimated quantity of each. And anthropologists were intensely interested in any clues that might help them to understand and reconstruct the civilization that many of them believed once flourished on the planet.

While preparing for the journey the crew received thousands of letters asking for information and giving suggestions. Many of the ideas were helpful, and all were given careful attention. Hundreds of the letters requested the crew to carry out various missions. Some of these were from institutions of higher learning, some from museums, some from educated and interested individuals—and some were from crackpots.

One letter in particular amused them. It was from a man who said he had difficulty with spelling and writing, but he had a very special reason for sending a letter, so he had struggled to write this one. He asked the crew to "keep an eye open for a fellow by the name of Hank Sylvester." Hank owed him thirty-seven dollars for a shotgun he had borrowed. Once the gun had been borrowed, Hank could not be found. He had disappeared. The letter continued:

"And doggonit, I've been lookin fer Hank all over these here mountings and never seen hide nor hair of him. Folks round about tell me you fellers are goin off to some new place or other. Now I wouldn be atall surprised if Hank is there, cause he sure ain't here. When you get wherever yore goin please look out fer Hank and fer my gun. And if you see the critter, tell him I'm still lookin fer them thirty seven dollars. If he don't pay or get that gun back to me right quick, you tell him I'm not goin to fool with him no more. I'm takin the law into my own hands, that's what I'm doin."

From that day "Hank" was blamed for everything that went wrong. If something was lost, it was Hank who had borrowed it. And if someone was missing from the location for any length of time, he would invariably excuse himself by saying that he was hunting for Hank. Had Hank known the troubles he was to be blamed for, he would have never taken the gun in the first place.

When the plans were made originally for the journey to Mars it was intended to have only two men aboard;

but these plans were altered to make a three-man crew. Three men would make it possible for any two of them to explore the surface of Mars while the third member remained in the ship to check the controls. If a calamity should befall the men outside the ship, the third member would be available to rescue them. Also it was believed that three men would make a happier crew, for there would always be a two-to-one vote, and decisions could be more easily reached. Most important, three persons would make the monotony easier to tolerate, for the ship would probably be air-borne for at least two months.

The leader of the three-man crew, and the first to be selected, was Dr. Charles Shallot, a remarkable person indeed. He was remarkable in many ways, not the least of which was his ability to understand the problems of other people and so become friendly with them. At first all the men stationed at the staging area stood in awe of his tremendous knowledge and courage. But they soon found that humility goes with greatness, and that the doctor was likable and easy to talk to. He was slight in build, energetic, and sharp-featured. He played an excellent game of golf, and was lively on the tennis court, although recently the demands on him left little time for relaxation. Even those who were close to him invariably estimated his age eight to ten years younger than his actual fifty-five years.

It was no accident that the leader of the expedition was

energetic, inspiring, and possessed of great learning. The
mission was the most hazardous ever attempted in the
history of man and perhaps the most important to his
future welfare, so the leader was selected only after the
most grueling trials, tests, and eliminations.

After rocket research had matured enough to carry out
the mission to the moon successfully, all branches of the
government became interested in its expansion. Heretofore only the armed forces were connected with it. But
now many agencies could see the advantages of expansion. They asked that the President and Congress establish
a nonmilitary commission to take over rocket research
and development. There was general accord with these
suggestions. Congress nominated a commission, and when
they named it they looked beyond the immediate present,
for they called it the Commission for Interplanetary Exploration. It was referred to as CIPE, a word composed of
the initial letters of the words in the title.

One of the first functions of the commission was to
compile a list of those scientists and engineers whose
knowledge and training might be of use to them. The list
included hundreds of names. After an intensive study of
the accomplishments of those who were on the roll, the
commission found that eight men were pioneering in the
field of rocket research and development. Dr. Shallot was
one of those eight.

The eight men received greetings from the President requesting their presence at the White House. The President explained that the commission needed the services of a highly trained scientist to direct the preparations for the journey into space, and to carry on investigations after landing on Mars. As a result of preliminary investigations the commission believed that the leader could be found from among these eight men. Would these men volunteer to be tested by the commission in an effort to determine who that leader should be?

Since all the scientists believed strongly in the future of rocket travel outside the gravitational field of the earth, they volunteered enthusiastically. But testing them was a difficult matter, for the field was so new that standards had not been established; in fact it was these men who were making those standards, and little was known about the personality and temperament needed. But it was possible to test them on the requirements needed for success in general. And tested they were.

The men were exposed to a series of heart-rending examinations that extended over a period of three months, and were designed to break down and eliminate all but the most perfectly qualified individuals.

First each man had to pass a severe physical examination. The men were placed in aviation training devices that simulated flight conditions and subjected them to dives, glides, climbs, and every conceivable maneuver. Electric contacts placed securely against the wrists and temples registered their reactions on a bank of indicators and on automatic recorders.

After they adjusted well enough to the conditions they might meet in ordinary flight the men were taken to the testing laboratories of what was the old Naval Academy at Annapolis, Maryland, where they were given a gravity test. Each man was put into an elevatorlike cage that rode up and down in a sealed cylindrical chamber. The elevator was raised rapidly, producing the effect of increasing the pull of gravity and duplicating the pressure conditions that would exist during the take-off and acceleration of a rocket. This test was repeated several times with the elevator rising faster and faster until the pressure was equivalent to four G's, which is four times the pull of gravity. Then the test went beyond this devastating level until the man being tested fainted. As in the flight test, reactions were measured and tabulated.

And there were other, more subtle tests that were performed at odd times. Doors were slammed loudly when the men were concentrating. Revolvers were fired behind their backs when they were lounging. Often when the men went to lunch the girls at the counter intentionally mixed up their orders. If a man ordered an egg sandwich he might get that kind or he might be handed chicken or ham on rye. The commission wanted to know how each would react in the face of irritation.

Invariably they were very nice about the errors. In many cases, it must be admitted, this was not because they were polite but because they were not aware of what they were eating, so engrossed were they in their work. But sometimes the reactions were far from calm.

Following the psychological tests the men were given a series of examinations on advanced theoretical mathematics. To take the tests they entered small, three-sided cubicles with the opened side behind them. They faced a blank wall, above which hung a small fluorescent lamp. Instructions were received over headphones that covered their ears snugly and blotted out all other sounds. As the instructions were given the men checked over the pencils, erasers, rulers, and slide rules that had been placed before them. The tests were given in four-hour stretches with intervals of one hour of rest. They were arranged in order of difficulty, each one being somewhat harder than the previous one. The tests became gradually so technical that only four men completed the tests satisfactorily.

These four rugged men, the best of whom were showing signs of strain, were then subjected to a trial that only the most stouthearted of men would agree to. They were stripped of all clothing and dressed in plain gray cotton pants, a matching shirt, and light canvas scuffs with no laces. The pants had no buttons or loops and there was no belt. The shirt also was buttonless. The men were blindfolded and their ears were plugged so they could not hear the noises of the city. They were led out of the building where they had been housed and placed in automobiles that rode them around for three hours so they would be absolutely lost. They were then returned to the building, although none of them knew it was the same one, and placed in separate rooms. An attendant told each of them to remove the blindfolds and ear plugs after three minutes had elapsed. This interval gave the attendant time to get out of the room and bolt the door.

When the blindfolds were removed, the sight the men saw was not pleasant. Each of them was in a small, dull room that had no windows and only one door that was fastened securely. The furniture in the room (it was more like a cell than a room) consisted of an unpainted wooden chair with a straight back and a board seat, a white metal cot, and a pail that was chained to a wall and which served as a toilet. The only other things in the cell were a small round basin with a cold water tap, a metal cup that was chained to the wall near the basin, a thin hard mattress and two blankets on the cot. These depressing surroundings were the prisons of the men for two full weeks. They were allowed nothing to read, nor anything with which they might write. They saw no persons at all, and the only sounds they heard were those of their own voice.

Meals were slipped into the cell through a locked slot at the bottom of the door. The meals were simple, and were served on tin plates with only a spoon with which to eat them.

Each man was watched closely through panels which provided one-way vision. The observers could see the man, but the man could not see the observers.

Here was slow torture of the mind. Men are active naturally. When they cannot express their feelings, exercise their bodies, or occupy their minds, insanity creeps in.

During the first two or three days the men slept or daydreamed, catching up on the sleep they had been promising themselves. They made the most of the luxury of having nothing to do. But strange things happened as the days wore on.

One of the men went mad. He sat in the straight-backed chair and methodically tore the blankets into long streamers about two inches wide. He draped the streamers about his head and over his shoulders, and then, with his eyes bulging from his head, he plunged underneath the cot.

The observers on the outside who had been watching all the time dragged him out finally, but he kicked and resisted every effort to help him. Fortunately he recovered when he was placed again in normal surroundings.

Like the others, Dr. Shallot spent the first day resting.
But while he was relaxed he developed a plan to help
him adjust to this trying situation, for he knew that he
would have to follow a routine to avoid fatigue.

He decided that a primary need would be exercise, so
when he arose from the hard, uncomfortable cot he did
twenty knee bends, counting them out loudly and rhyth-
mically. He then did push-ups and body twists until he
perspired freely. He bathed as best he could with the
limited facilities. The doctor had been a scrupulously
clean person, so the hardship of bathing in cold water
from a sink not much larger than a saucepan was difficult
to bear. His beard grew profusely. He had never before
gone unshaven. At first, when his beard was little more
than a stubble, it itched unmercifully, but as the hair
grew longer it became softer and did not bother him.

For relaxation he played mental chess with an imaginary opponent. This was a tremendous exertion, for not
only did he have to remember the entire board of sixty-
four squares, but he had also to keep in mind the position
of thirty-two pieces, sixteen white and sixteen black. This
high degree of concentration enabled him to escape from
his surroundings, so his activity was restful.

The cell became more abominable as the days dragged
by. The pail that served as a toilet was chained to the

wall, and it was usually emptied while he slept. But there came a time when the pail was cleaned no longer, and the odor in the small, windowless room was nauseating. This was only another test. Perhaps a man could withstand solitary confinement when conditions were somewhat favorable; but the commission wanted to know what would happen to a man when all the cards were stacked against him. Dr. Shallot helped the situation by filling the pail with water. Although the water did not neutralize the odor, it lessened it considerably.

He knew that a certain time must be allotted to various activities. Since he had no watch, he had to devise some method of keeping track of time. He decided that he could do it by regulating the flow of water into the basin. He reduced the flow until the water dripped slowly, and he then caught the drops in the tin cup. While the water dripped he counted sixty seconds, saying one thousand between each number: one, one thousand, two, one thousand, three, and so on. By counting slowly in this manner he found that the cup filled in forty minutes. Since he could measure time, even though the manner was crude, he could divide the day into periods of work, play, eating, exercising, and resting.

For work the doctor gave detailed talks on astrophysics to imaginary classes. He used the same inflections of tone, and the same postures that he would have used had he been in the lecture hall back on the Columbia University campus. He organized his information in this field and tabulated it mentally into logical, sequential lectures. As he lectured, he would turn to the imaginary blackboard and place series of equations upon it. The lecture periods were each one hundred minutes long with a ten-minute break, and only one was given each day.

These work periods were followed by additional exercise. His friends had been teasing the doctor for some time past because he was unable to bend over and touch the floor with his hands while keeping his knees straight. He decided to do something about this, and practiced religiously every day. At the end of the two weeks he could just touch, although he was at least four inches short of the floor when he started. He set up many other obstacles to be mastered, such as lowering himself to the floor while standing on one foot and rising again without touching anything.

Dr. Shallot followed his routine carefully and made the most of his imprisonment, as he did of every situation where he happened to find himself. When he came out he was a better chess player than when he went in. He could bend over and touch the floor without bending his knees, an ability he never lost afterwards, for he kept practicing. In fact, as he himself said, he was able to get more exercise in his prison cell than he usually got in his own laboratory. And the doctor had organized his information on astrophysics so well that he was an encyclopedia of facts and data in that field.

The results of the many tests were overwhelmingly in Dr. Shallot's favor. The commission selected him to direct the mission, but before the news could be flashed to the world there remained one last hurdle to be passed. This was the doctor's family. No man can do his best or devote all his energies to a cause unless those close to him approve of what he is doing. And approval alone is not enough. There must be encouragement and enthusiastic interest. Without the scientist's knowledge his wife was interviewed to determine what her attitude would be should her husband be given this responsibility. She realized how great an honor the post was and, in spite of the dangers involved in the mission, all of which were fully explained to her, she gave her unqualified consent and support.

Thus Dr. Charles Shallot, a native of California, now a resident of White Plains, New York, research scientist and professor of rockets and jets at Columbia University, became the leader of the first long-range rocket flight ever attempted by man. And now he was air-borne in the *Lodestar*, completely unconscious and unaware of the hurtling speed of the ship he was commanding.

A<small>T THE STAGING AREA</small>, the deafening, fearsome roar of the take-off made way for heavy subsonic vibrations that chattered one's teeth and grated one's bones. And then a great silence crept over the huge bowl, its very softness seeming to respect the prayers of the people assembled there.

There was silence in the *Lodestar* too. In 2½ minutes the rocket had left the earth's atmosphere. Although the auxiliary rockets were spewing hot gases they made no sound, for there was nothing to carry vibrations. After twenty seconds had elapsed the nuclear jet went into action.

When the main jet operated, the acceleration increased. The crew had fainted when the acceleration reached slightly over four G's, shortly after the ship was off the ground. But they were to be subjected to still more strain.

54

Their slumped bodies, held securely in the bucket seats by the restraining belts, gasped for air. And under closed eyelids their eyeballs rolled upward. The ship hurtled toward the zenith until the auxiliary rockets were spent. When these no longer provided any thrust they fell away from the ship. As this occurred, an automatic mechanism tilted the ship slightly toward the east so it could utilize any effect caused by the rotation of the earth.

As the *Lodestar* moved farther out into the rare gases of space it accelerated more easily. For eight minutes the main jet blasted at full power, crushing the crew within the ship. Finally it reached escape velocity, the speed required if an object is to escape from the earth's gravitational field. The *Lodestar* was careening through the heavens at seven miles a second.

When it reached escape velocity the jet closed down automatically. It did not shut off completely but maintained enough acceleration to preserve a gravitational field within the ship itself.

Because Jack Strong was the youngest crew member, he was the first to recover from shock, and from the devastating pressure of the acceleration. His eyelids raised heavily, only to fall again. His hands and forearms moved sluggishly, as though they were encased in lead gauntlets. He raised his head with great effort, only to have it fall forward against the spring band that prevented it from rolling loosely. But once recovery began, it proceeded rapidly, and in a few moments Jack's eyes were opened and he was looking around him.

Jack had played football in high school. He was too short and light to be on the varsity team, but he enjoyed the intramural play. There had been many times when he was tackled so hard and piled upon so much that he came out dazed, almost punch drunk. He felt the same way now.

It took him a minute to realize where he was. When he regained his wits, his first concern was for his crew mates, who were still unconscious. He was tempted to unstrap himself to go to their aid; but each of them had been instructed to sit tight until all had recovered, or until fifteen minutes had elapsed.

So Jack remained in his seat. He unfastened the one belt that buckled his knees to his chest, but the main straps he left secured. He stretched his legs before him and gazed at the instrument panel. When he focused his eyes on the dials his head spun and waves of nausea spread over him. He closed his eyes quickly and pressed his forehead into the V made by his thumb and first finger. He pushed hard against his hand and then rubbed his brow heavily. After a few moments of massage he could feel strength flowing through him as his blood circulated more regularly. The nausea and spinning were replaced by a light-headed feeling.

Jack opened his eyes again and stared at the instruments. Since the attitude of the ship had changed and since the bucket seat had enabled him to swing freely, the panel was now directly in front of him instead of over his head. It now formed the front end of the crew compartment and dominated it. The needle of the radiation indicator shivered at a point slightly above medium and jumped into the high zone occasionally. This was to be expected, for the reactor was decreasing its activity, and whenever this happened there were bursts of high-level energy before the action leveled off.

Two green lights blinked on and off, indicating that the course selector and stabilizer, which was essentially an automatic pilot, was functioning. The bubble of the horizontal axis indicator was to the left of center, which meant that the ship was tilted slightly in the opposite direction.

Other than this the instruments showed a trim ship. The timer which controlled the automatic devices ticked away loudly. It had started the main jet at the proper time, then tilted the *Lodestar* while her crew was unconscious. It resounded against the soft purr made by the generators, instrument rotors, and gyro rotors.

Jack struggled to overpower a fear that gnawed its way into his thoughts. He hoped for the quick recovery of his crew mates so he could get rid of the intense loneliness that was sweeping over him.

He could feel no motion. The human body cannot feel velocity and so, just as a train passenger is not aware of his motion (unless he looks out a window), Jack was aware of none, although he was plummeting through space at 25,000 miles an hour. For that matter, he would not have known he was air-borne had there been no instruments to tell him so.

Jack heard a deep-throated groan from Mr. Warick. He turned his head quickly to see him. "Mr. Warick, Don," he called, but there was no response. Jack contemplated unbuckling himself to go to Don's aid, but just then Mr. Warick lifted his right arm wearily and rubbed his brow.

Jack called again, "Mr. Warick, Don, can you hear me?"

Mr. Warick showed no sign of hearing, so Jack called louder.

This time Mr. Warick heard. He turned his head toward Jack, but he could not see his friend for he was rubbing his eyes and brow as though he had a severe headache.

"We made it, Mr. Warick," Jack shouted. "We're way out in space; more than a thousand miles out already."

Poor Mr. Warick was trying hard to focus his bleary eyes.

"We what?" he asked slowly and quietly with the jumbled incoherence of a man emerging from ether.

"We're out in space. We're air-borne and in free flight."

This made an impression, for Jack could see Mr. Warick's eyes brighten. He was regaining his senses.

"I must have been unconscious." He spoke thickly as he rubbed his brow, cheeks, and chin. Jack smiled at his bewilderment.

"You sure have been," Jack agreed.

"How long?" he asked.

"More than ten minutes."

"Ten minutes," he exclaimed. "You're fooling. Why, I've never been out like that in my whole life. Even when they gave us those acceleration tests, I was out for only a minute or so. Ten minutes," he shook his head, "I can't believe it. I still feel shaky. How about you, Jack? You look as though you made out all right."

"I'm fine. I was out, too, but I've been conscious for several minutes, waiting for someone to come to and keep me company."

Mr. Warick looked closely at Dr. Shallot. "The boss doesn't look too good to me," he said to Jack with concern. And he didn't, for his muscles were completely relaxed, allowing his cheeks to hang loosely, and the usual ruddiness of his features was blanched. "There's nothing we can do, though," continued Mr. Warick. "We'll have to wait till he recovers."

"I guess so," said Jack. "We'll have to wait another five minutes anyway. If he doesn't show any signs of recovery by twelve fifteen we'll unstrap and go to his aid."

They checked the clock on the instrument panel. The time was exactly eleven minutes after twelve, earth time. They kept their eyes on the doctor, much concerned about his uneven respiration.

As they waited, Jack spoke. "You know, even though space is all around us and spreading to eternity, I feel that I could reach out and touch the tips of it." Mr. Warick grunted, and Jack let his thoughts wander. "You might say that the *Lodestar* is our universe instead of all that out there." He moved his arm toward the bulkheads of the ship.

As Jack spoke he gazed at the instrument panel of the ship.

Mr. Warick was content to listen, since he wasn't fully recovered, so Jack continued talking.

"I keep looking at that radionic computer," he said, "and even though I know the thing is accurate, I just can't believe it. Now it says we've covered almost 3,000 miles. That means we're going about 25,000 miles an hour. It seems to me that we're standing still. How does it feel to you, Mr. Warick? Do you feel any motion? Doesn't it seem to you that we're floating in space?"

"You're right," said Mr. Warick, his senses perking up. "It does seem as if we were floating. It surely doesn't seem that we can be going very fast. And it's so quiet, Jack. I never believed anything could be so soundless."

As they talked together they watched the doctor, as a mother watches an ailing child.

"I'm worried about him," said Jack with concern.

"I don't think you need to be. He doesn't look too good; but you remember that he was slow to recover from the test blackouts. After all, he's quite a bit older than we are, and he can't pick up as rapidly."

As Mr. Warick was speaking, Jack noticed that Dr. Shallot was moving his head back and forth slowly.

"He's coming to," Jack said excitedly.

Dr. Shallot recovered slowly. When he was still dazed but conscious enough to hear, they asked him if he wanted a stimulant. He shook his head no. He preferred to revive naturally and slowly rather than chance an additional tax on his heart.

When he had recovered fully, the crew discussed their progress to the moment, removed the protective webbing from in front of the panel, and made instrument readings so they could orient themselves.

Then Dr. Shallot maneuvered the ship until the bubble

of the horizontal axis indicator moved to the center of the tube and the *Lodestar* was in level flight.

The speed indicator was not fixed for continuous reading as this would cause friction and drag, so it had to be placed in position before a reading could be made. He did this remotely by opening a small vent toward the nose of the ship. As the air raced by the gauge, it caused a pointer to move over a dial. (Some people believed that there is no air at this altitude. Although there is none, in the sense of the atmosphere of the earth, there are enough molecules present to activate certain mechanisms, such as the speed calculator. It was found that there are as many as three molecules per cubic centimeter of space, which is more than the single molecule that many astrophysicists believed to be the maximum.) The exact reading of the space rocket, taken at 12:30 P.M. earth time, was 25,520 miles per hour, which was fast enough to go all the way around the earth at the equator in sixty minutes. This was approximately the velocity they had anticipated at this stage of the journey.

The men watched the temperature dials closely. They were especially concerned about the one that measured the temperature of the outer skin of the ship. It was essential that this temperature be known at all times, for the skin might become so hot that it would melt off before anyone realized what was happening. This gauge, and the mechanism it operated, were on manual control during the checking period. During the initial stage of the flight it was on automatic control, and it was normally kept there.

If the ship became too hot, a thermostatic control started to operate the refrigerating equipment, which kept operating until the temperature held at a steady 70 degrees. If the ship became too cold, as it might when going through certain elevations and regions of the universe, heating equipment took over and maintained the temperature at which the control dial had been set. The *Lodestar* was equipped with a heating-refrigerating apparatus that would change the temperature as many as ten degrees a minute either upward or downward. Atomic energy from the prime power source did this.

The heating was done by circulating a medium composed of a molten-rock derivative, which was combined with a solvent to keep it in a semiliquid condition. This material was used because of its high specific heat, because it was noncorrosive, and because it was comparatively light, even though the basic material in it was rock.

Just inside the outer skin of the ship was a narrow space filled with a maze of tubes, some of which carried this heating medium. The molten-rock derivative was circulated through a section of the nuclear reactor where its temperature was raised, and then it was pumped through these tubes. The temperature gauge on the panel was steady at 70 degrees, which meant that the temperature control mechanism was functioning properly.

Pipes carrying a refrigerant were interlaced with the heat tubes. The refrigerating mechanism was much like that in conventional home refrigerators, since it had a compressor and an evaporator, although the evaporator was much more extensive. Like the heating mechanism, this apparatus was also powered with energy derived from the atomic reactor, although the relationship was less direct. A tube containing ordinary air passed into the reactor. This air was heated to a high temperature, and it was then pumped to a highly efficient, small, and powerful gas turbine. Connected to this turbine was a compact electric generator that could produce 1500 watts of power, yet its actual weight was only fifty-eight pounds. Some of the electricity thus generated was used to operate the compressor, which was the heart of the cooling system. All the electricity used throughout the ship came from this generator, and this same mechanism would provide the power required after the ship had landed at its destination.

Since there was no fuel but the small amount contained in the nuclear reactor, there was no fuel gauge. The reactor was regenerative; that is, a large percentage of the fuel was used over and over again. Ultimately the reaction would become contaminated with waste products and it would cease; but the original fuel would last a long time. Although the metal employed was plutonium, uranium 235 could have been used, as also could thorium. Plutonium proved to be the most satisfactory substance in all the tests from which the *Lodestar* had evolved.

It was the function of the plutonium to provide power for the ship to get into space and to its destination, as well as back again; once there it was to provide the heat and light needed to maintain comfort and perhaps life itself. It was to furnish the power to run the refrigeration equipment, and all the other electrical devices and appliances that were integral parts of the apparatus. This vast amount of power was to be supplied by only a small chunk of plutonium. The three cases Jack had picked up at the supply depot contained little more than a quart of pure plutonium, yet this was more than enough to supply all the energy the ship required.

Dr. Shallot was checking the other instruments, and found everything in good order. Since all the equipment was working well, the crew turned next to the problem of setting their course accurately.

The flight started in June and would last for two months. The course of the *Lodestar* and the date of its departure had been computed in such a way that it would approach its goal when Mars was in a position closest to earth. In August of 1988 it would be only 35,400,000 miles away from earth instead of 50,000,000 miles which is its average distance.

Dr. Shallot laid out a large plotting board which had been folded into the base of the instrument panel. He was scribing lines upon it, measuring angles, and making numerous notations. All the while he mumbled to himself as he checked and rechecked his figures with a cylindrical slide rule.

Mr. Warick and Jack looked on intently, but kept quiet so they would not disturb Dr. Shallot. Mr. Warick was a good navigator but Jack knew little about it. To him the subject of astrogation (navigation in space) was a deep mystery. He knew little more than the fundamentals that he learned as part of his three-months specialized training that followed his selection by CIPE.

After much deliberation, Dr. Shallot said, "There men, I think that does it. Here's the course."

He switched on a microfilm projector which threw a map of the heavens onto a fluorescent screen.

"I have just checked the findings of the Palomar observatory to make sure, and Mars will be right here in sixty days."

As he spoke he pointed to Betelgeuse, shoulder star of the constellation Orion. His years of teaching made him sound a little pedantic as he explained what he was doing.

"Our problem," he continued, "is to regulate our speed and direction so that we and Mars will reach the same spot at the same time."

While the *Lodestar* was hurtling toward Mars, the planet was moving some 75,000 miles an hour in its orbit around the sun. The problem, therefore, involved enormous velocities.

"That takes a neat bit of figuring," said Jack. "If we were going slow, it wouldn't be so hard; but when both you and your target are moving along at thousands of miles an hour it's a different story."

"It would seem so but the problem is the same. You use the same method, whether you're going fast or slow. The only difference is the size of the figures."

Then Mr. Warick said jokingly, "That's a new face you just made, Jack. I never saw that one before."

Jack grinned sheepishly and said nothing. Dr. Shallot and Mr. Warick smiled good naturedly at his discomfort.

Since childhood Jack had had a habit of screwing his face into weird contortions whenever he was puzzled. Sometimes a corner of his mouth was raised abruptly, or his brows might be furrowed into deep lines; but no matter what the contortion might be, Mr. Warick invariably noticed it and teased the boy.

Jack straightened his face as Dr. Shallot said, "Now we'll line up the ship with our objective."

There were four red buttons in the formation of a square in front of the doctor, each of which regulated a small steering jet. He pushed the lower right-hand button and then the one on the upper left. As he pushed the buttons, he watched a screen which showed the movements of a miniature *Lodestar* over a replica of the sky. When he was satisfied with the flight stability, he set the automatic pilot in operation. This was a small box containing gyroscopes that were spun at a regular rate by electrical impulses. One gyroscope kept the nose from rising or falling, and the other one kept the ship from veering to port or starboard. Now that their course was set and the automatic pilot was adjusted, the *Lodestar* could continue to accelerate to top speed.

The speed control was moved forward.

"Now we can relax," said Dr. Shallot as he unloosened the main stabilizing belt, "for it will take some time to speed up to our greatest velocity. Let's hope we can reach thirty thousand miles an hour. If we can, we'll meet Mars as we planned; otherwise we shall have to make a new flight plan."

"Thirty thousand miles an hour, wow!" said Mr. Warick. "If we should meet anyone out for a Sunday drive, I hope he blows his horn. It would be quite a smash if we hit anything at that speed."

Although both Dr. Shallot and Jack laughed, it was

more at the way Mr. Warick spoke than at the words he said, for a smashup would indeed be the end of all of them.

As they laughed, Mr. Warick unbuckled his retaining belts and said, "Come on, you two, let's take a look at earth. At the speed we're going, we'll soon be unable to see any details. Let's see if the folks back there are missing us."

MR. WARICK put his eye to the peep sight. He moved a small lever that was recessed in the bulkhead at waist height and turned the sight through 360 degrees. Through long hours of tedious attention to engineering details he had learned to rest at every opportunity. As he moved the lever his body was relaxed; but when earth hove into his field of vision his legs stiffened, his shoulders hunched, for this was a sight of rare beauty.

"Marvelous," he exclaimed softly with the awed surprise of one who sees a masterpiece for the first time. "It's the most beautiful thing I've ever seen."

He would not take his eyes from the sight. He was transfixed, spellbound by the panorama of the heavens.

After some time Dr. Shallot asked, "Can you see Hank anywhere down there, Don? Or what *do* you see that is so fascinating?"

Mr. Warick took the hint and turned the sight over to his colleague. "No," he said, "I can't see Hank or any sign of him, but there's plenty of beauty to look at."

Mr. Warick was telling Jack of the view he had seen. This only served to heighten the boy's impatience to see the view. Finally his turn came.

Jack had seen globes of all kinds, first in his classroom in grammar school, then in high school, and almost constantly since joining the mission. He thought he knew what the earth in space would look like. But the glorious, breath-taking spectacle far surpassed what he had imagined. It made him gasp and covered his body with shivers. There was a majesty about the earth when seen as a whole that was many fold greater than the beauty of its parts.

The earth was a massive thing. Jack could see the area of the entire United States and much more, for the northern and southern fringes of the continent of North America were becoming apparent rapidly. The Pacific Ocean shone with a gemlike brilliance, and parts of it caught the sunlight as would a huge mirror.

Jack could not discern the desert area just east of the Rockies from which the *Lodestar* had embarked. But he could see the rugged nature of the mountains running like vertebrae along the body of the western part of the continent. And he could see that the western part of the mountains was in brilliant sunlight while on the eastern side shadows were beginning to show.

Jack had been in planes ever since he could walk, and yet he had never reached a height great enough to show the curvature of the earth. Now he could see it clearly. The land masses sloped away just as though they were part of a ball, which, of course, they actually were.

He was carried away by the panorama spread before him; the soft greens of the forest areas blended into the neutral tans of the plains, and a pale blue tenuous veil covered all.

Mr. Warick nudged Jack. "Can you see your home town, Jack?"

"Almost, Mr. Warick." Jack was serious. Mr. Warick was joking.

After looking a moment or two longer, Jack continued, "Really though, I think I can make out New York and Philadelphia. I'm sure I can see Chicago."

"No doubt about it, Jack," agreed Dr. Shallot. "Those darker areas are the cities. You can see St. Louis, San Francisco, and New Orleans too if you look at the right places."

"Anyone who thought Columbus was mad when he said the world was round should be here," said Jack. "If they took one squint through this sight, they could see in a moment how right he was."

Gazing out at the earth, watching the changing colors of it, and the shadows moving across it became a favorite pastime. It never ceased to hold interest, even after the *Lodestar* was so far away that details could be seen no longer. In fact, interest became greater in direct proportion to the increasing distance from the earth. It was home to the crew and, as each passing moment carried them farther away, each member was anxious for a lingering glance, one which might well be his last.

A few hours later the entire earth was visible. A soft line blended the lighted part and that which was in darkness. It hung in space, spotlighted by the sun so brilliantly that it stood out strongly against its backdrop of deepest black—a black that was all the deeper because of the myriad of bright stars that were sprinkled through it. The crew observed the rotation of the earth and watched sections emerge from darkness into light. You couldn't see both happening at the same time, any more than we can see it on the moon. But within the ship itself, and in the universe immediately around it, there was no day and night; nothing but constant, deep darkness. Light came from the sun alone, and there was no reflected light for there was nothing from which it could be mirrored.

"What time is it?" asked Mr. Warick who was making an entry in the log book.

On earth it was a fairly simple matter to keep track of

time. When the sun rose everyone knew another day had dawned. All one needed to do was count these risings to orient himself in time. But in the *Lodestar* there was no such aid. Unless some check were maintained, time as it is known on earth would have no meaning.

Jack glanced at the time section of the instrument panel. "1650 I make it, Mr. Warick."

Time was reckoned on the twenty-four-hour system which had come into wide usage. In this system the hours were counted from midnight to midnight. One in the afternoon became 1300 and so on until 2400 was reached. 1650 meant that it was 4:50, or ten minutes to five.

Jack studied the time section more carefully. It was a series of dials activated by mechanisms that were geared together. The pointer or the first dial moved rapidly, for this was calibrated in seconds. When it made a complete rotation it caused the dial next to it to move one notch. This was the minute hand. When this moved around completely, it clocked sixty minutes and moved a third dial, the hour hand, one notch. One rotation of this hand indicated the passage of twenty-four hours. Weeks, months and even years as reckoned on earth were recorded in this same manner.

Not content with this mechanism, which was foolproof in its construction and operation, Dr. Shallot always recorded the passage of days in a black notebook which was as much a part of him as a mitt is part of a first baseman.

"How come you check off the days in your book?" asked Mr. Warick one day. He pointed at the time dials on the panel. "That mechanism up there won't let us down. It's better than any ticker ever made."

"I know that, Don," said the doctor. "It's just a habit I have. It's one of those things I feel I must do every day, like brushing my teeth, or else I'm uncomfortable."

It was fortunate that Dr. Shallot had this peculiar habit, for it was to prove of great value.

When you go up in an airplane you have a feeling of possessiveness and power. You are lord of all you survey. But even though you are above the earth and free to move up, down, or sideways, you still feel that you are a part of the earth. There is an unconscious feeling of comfort in the fact that if you cut the power you will settle down to earth and to home.

There was no such feeling in the *Lodestar*. There was no bond with earth; for that matter there was no bond with anything. The ship and her crew were an insignificant spot of matter in the endless reaches of the universe, just as were the meteors and lesser heavenly bodies. And in the same way that these meteors flashed through the heavens, the *Lodestar* was speeding through space.

The excitement that had been building up during the days preceding the take-off, and which had reached a peak earlier in the day, was now tapering off. The muscles, minds, and nerves of the crew were relaxing to produce fatigue and a gnawing, demanding hunger. Jack's stomach was the first to feel the surge of emptiness.

"I'm hungry," he said as he pushed on his empty stomach. "Let's make our first meal aboard something to remember."

"It'll be something to remember all right, Jack," said Mr. Warick, "but not because it's so delicious."

As he spoke, Mr. Warick, who was nearest to the food locker, started to prepare the meal. The locker was opened by snapping back a section of the foam-rubber lining of the compartment. A table and two narrow benches jack-knifed out of the bulkhead to disclose an extensive larder of dehydrated and concentrated foods. By using this type of food it was possible to store provisions for several months in a space six feet square and a foot and a half deep. The original plans called for the use of frozen foods, which would have been more palatable; but the space saved by taking only the less tasty dried foods made their use imperative.

Adjacent to this compartment was a section that contained an electric stove, a water tap, and the few utensils that were essential.

"What will you have gentlemen?" asked Mr. Warick

with a flourish. "Will it be steaks, lamb chops, or perhaps you prefer some toasty-brown fried chicken."

"Don't kid about it," said Jack despairingly. "It's going to be hard enough to eat nothing but dried foods without being reminded of luscious things like that."

"I guess you're right, Jack. All we can do is open package number 1 and hope there's something good in it." Mr. Warick reached for the package. "While I'm opening this, put on some water for the brogerm, Jack."

Brogerm was a health beverage that consisted of concentrated meat broth and the oils extracted from wheat germ. It was a poor substitute for the coffee that Dr. Shallot liked so well, but a necessary one, for it not only replaced coffee as a beverage but it was also highly nutritious. The staple foods in the locker were boxed in numbered cases. The foods for the first meal were in case number 1, those for the second meal in case number 2, and so on. By this method no one knew what foods would be served, so there was always a feeling of expectancy and curiosity at meal time.

Mr. Warick broke the package into four sections as directed, and handed one of them to Jack.

Jack read the directions. "It says to place this in the pressure cooker with four cups of water. Do you suppose that means wrapper and all?"

"I imagine so, Jack. I think the wrappers are edible. They're plant cellulose and can be digested easily."

Jack gave the package to Mr. Warick, and then read the directions on the other three. "These three go into the hydrator."

He placed the three packages inside an ovenlike device. He pushed a button which allowed steam to enter. This caused the foods to assume their normal size and shape in a few minutes.

"I couldn't tell what anything was, could you?" asked Jack.

"I can't be sure, Jack," answered Mr. Warick. "But the one package is carrots, if I remember correctly. At least that's the way carrots looked when we were on concentrates a few months ago."

"Those sure were rough times," said Jack.

Jack and Mr. Warick were referring to the one-month training period held six months ago when the three of them lived together under conditions similar to those existing within the *Lodestar*.

The relief valve on the pressure cooker popped off and Mr. Warick removed it from the stove.

Dr. Shallot had been busy at the plotting board but he became interested in food when he heard the buzzer. He stepped to the stove and removed the cover of the cooker.

"Hmm, smells like split pea soup, Don. I hope it's as good as it smells."

In a few moments the hydrator shut off and Jack removed the food that was now returned to its original shape, thoroughly cooked. The meal consisted of brogerm (as did every meal), pea soup, carrots, potatoes, sliced beef, and a biscuit impregnated with butter dots.

"That wasn't bad at all," said Mr. Warick as he drank the last of his brogerm. "I've tasted worse."

"It's not too bad," Jack agreed grudgingly, "but I doubt if I'll ever get used to it."

"Oh, you'll get used to it, Jack." Mr. Warick turned to Dr. Shallot. "You know, Doctor, I believe I'm going to like this brogerm. It has a flavor all its own."

"Yes, Don, but I'll take coffee, thank you."

"Well," Mr. Warick laughed, "you two had better get used to this food, or else I'll be eating so much and getting so fat I won't be able to move out of the ship."

Cleaning up after the meal was a simple matter. All the soiled dishes and utensils were clipped into the square-sided sink and the panel covering it was secured tightly. When a valve was opened, hot water and steam sprayed over the utensils, cleaning and sterilizing them. The water from the washer was piped into a distiller that double distilled the water, and from there it was pumped back into the storage tanks located between the inner and outer bulkheads.

They were far from certain that water would be found on Mars, so they used water very carefully, to extend the supply to the utmost. Because of its great weight and bulk not much could be stored, so every drop was reclaimed. All wash water was distilled, as was also urine. Fecal wastes were broken down by chemical action, and reduced to a fraction of the original bulk.

The *Lodestar* had been cruising for several hours, building up its velocity slowly but constantly. The silence within the ship was absolute. Since the nuclear reactor made no noise whatever, there were no engine noises. The centrifugal pumps and generators were not fastened to the body of the ship directly, but were insulated from it. If they were not, the whir of the rotors would carry into the crew compartment and set up a whine that would have become unbearable. The *Lodestar* was surrounded by blackness and silence. It was as if it were wrapped in many thicknesses of heavy, black velvet through which neither light nor sounds could penetrate.

The crew would be air-borne for two months, cooped up in their small, soundless compartment. For many men this would have meant as many days of boredom and monotony, since no one could go out for a stroll around the deck, go for a swim in the pool, or get away from the other crew members for the least instant. But much care and time had been taken in the selection of the *Lodestar's* crew, and it was trained to be compatible. Whatever flaws of personality adjustment there might have been were corrected during the training period.

After the evening meal the crew relaxed.

"I'll challenge you to a game of chess," Jack said to Mr. Warick.

"Challenge accepted," he replied as he sat back in Dr. Shallot's flight chair. When they were relaxing the crew sat in whichever chair seemed convenient. "But let it be on your own head."

Jack went to a small compartment from which he removed a light steel tube. The tube was made of narrow sections fastened together like the cover of a roll-top desk. He unrolled the tube to make a chess board, and within the tube were two narrow bar magnets which he placed beneath the board to hold it rigid. He placed chess men on the board. These were held to it by small alnico magnets embedded in the base of each man.

Mr. Warick and Jack swung their chairs about so they faced each other, and then locked them in position. Mr. Warick won the white so he moved first. He moved his king pawn two squares, Jack parried by bringing out his queen knight, and the game was on.

As the game progressed Dr. Shallot decided to do some

reading. He reached to the base of the instrument panel and pulled on a small thumb tab. A microfilm projector cantilevered into chair-high position. The doctor placed a film in the projector, swung his chair around to face the rear of the compartment and projected the first frame on a twenty-four inch square screen that had swung into position as the projector was moved upward. He relaxed in his seat and changed frames with a flick of his finger. By the use of these microfilms the contents of a large book filled only one cubic inch of space. Thus an extensive library of technical books, fiction, travel, and biography was contained in less space than that required for three ordinary volumes.

And so passed a pleasant evening. Weariness crept over the crew one by one. When Dr. Shallot suggested that they should be getting some rest there were none who disagreed. But until they were well on their way the sleeping was to be done in shifts, so that one person was always awake. Jack and Mr. Warick were persuaded to take the first six hours while the leader kept watch.

The beds were sections of the foam rubber lining of the compartment which were loosened and placed on the floor. Mr. Warick and Jack lay down and the doctor fastened stabilizing straps over them loosely. These would prevent their being thrown, should the ship change course suddenly.

As they were settling down, Jack said, "We have plenty to dream about tonight, but I'm so tired that I think I'll sleep like a log."

Mr. Warick agreed. Then he asked Dr. Shallot, "Are you sure you'll be all right? Wouldn't you prefer that I take the first shift?"

"No, no," said Dr. Shallot in a tone that did not invite argument. "Of course I'll be all right." He sensed that he was being abrupt. He smiled, then, and added, "Unless our friend Hank Sylvester is roaming around out there with his shotgun." He continued seriously, "You two had better stop worrying about me and get some sleep. Six hours will go by quickly."

"Right you are, Doctor," said Don as he and Jack stretched luxuriously and settled down to rest.

EVEN THOUGH he was exhausted, sleep did not come to Jack quickly. Through arduous months he had been conditioned to space travel; but it took effort to feel comfortable in the small compartment that had become his world, surrounded by nothing but dark, soundless space.

The honor and glory that went with the mission were pleasing to him, but such things gave little comfort. Assurance had to come from his comrades and from confidence in their ability as well as his own. Whenever doubts of success inched their way into his consciousness he had only to recall the accomplishments of Dr. Shallot and Mr. Warick to be reassured.

As Jack lay upon his air mattress his thoughts left the ship and traveled back to earth. He thought of his mother and father, and wondered what they were doing and what they were thinking. He smiled to himself as he remembered the happy way his father's objections to his career in science were overcome.

Jack's father was the manager of a small clothing store, and he had always hoped that Jack would come into the business with him when he was finished with school. Mr. Strong was a stickler for exactness and neatness at all times and in all things. More than once he had scolded Jack for being careless. During one of these times he first showed his disapproval of Jack's interest in science.

Jack remembered clearly.

"Jack," his father had called loudly in a menacing tone, "come up here at once."

Jack ran up the stairs. His father was standing in the doorway of Jack's room, his hands on his hips. He was looking into the room.

"I don't know why you drag all this junk in here, Jack. There's no sense in cluttering a place with rocks, and leaves, and pieces of wood. A room is a place to sleep in and not a place to drop everything you happen to put your hands on."

"But, Dad, it's—"

"No buts about it, Jack. I won't have a mess like this."

Jack's shoulders sagged.

"It won't do you any good to look like a sick dog. You'll have to clean it up, throw the stuff out or put it away somewhere. Clear it up any way you want to."

Jack's mother overheard his father. She waited at the bottom of the stairs for him to come down. Jack heard her say, "The boy should be allowed to do as he wants to in his own room. He'll clean it up if you give him a reason for doing so."

"All I see in there is bugs and rocks and leaves, and goodness knows what else. If it isn't a frog that he has up there, it's a snake or some other fool thing that he's found."

"Those are the things that he likes," said his mother softly.

"That's just the trouble. Why can't he like his school work instead of those things? His marks are a disgrace."

His mother had to admit that the marks were not satisfactory. "But he's good in science," she said hopefully. "He does very well in that."

The undercurrent of conflict between Jack's interests and his father's hopes ran for many years. When Jack was a sophomore in high school, his science teacher was amazed at his ability.

"Mr. Strong," he said to Jack's father, "I'm convinced that Jack has unusual ability in the field of science. Would you mind if I give him extra help, for I think he can go far. Industry is looking for boys like him."

This was the decision that Jack's father had sensed, but which he had been side-stepping as long as he could. If he agreed, the hopes he had had for years would be over. If he did not agree, Jack would be turned against him.

"It's a hard thing you're asking of me," he said falteringly, "it's much harder than you think. Ever since Jack was a youngster I've had plans for him, and this isn't one of them." Then he smiled ironically. "But what can I do? If he's so able, I can't stand in his way."

"Good," said his teacher, "you'll not regret this decision."

This was a turning point in Jack's life. From time to time his family received glowing reports from his science teachers. The reports from his other teachers, especially English and Latin, were still not so bright. In fact, they were often very dull.

But Jack's father encouraged him in every way he could, for after his first disappointment he was immensely pleased with his son's progress. As Jack fell asleep in the *Lodestar* he could feel the warm handshake, and hear the husky words of his father. "Good luck, my boy," he had said. "Your mother and I are real proud of you; just as proud as we can be." These simple words, spoken with sincerity, were treasured above all the flowery praises of the speechmakers and government emissaries.

When Jack awakened, he prepared breakfast and then studied astrogation. The sleep periods were part of a rigid routine that was followed the first six weeks of the air journey. There was a work period in both the morning and the afternoon, during which the crew studied. Jack learned astronavigation from the doctor—not the elementary type needed by a navigator; but the advanced form required of physicists and researchers. Mr. Warick studied history and became an expert on the ancient Romans.

The day was broken with social periods during which the crew played chess, watched films, listened to music recorded on wire, and discussed their views on Mars and what they expected to find when they got there. The meals were not interesting, although they were nutritious. Jack's enjoyment of them was not helped by his dreaming of the apple pies and roast chickens that his mother could prepare so expertly. Usually the hours slipped by rapidly, although there were times when they dragged and seemed endless.

At the end of the sixth week, details on the earth were visible no longer. On the whole the planet came to look more and more like Mars or Venus when they are viewed from the earth.

Space was nothing but darkness. The stars were bright crystals glistening constantly in a sea of somber black, a beautiful sight to see. Since there was no atmosphere in space to reflect sunlight, they saw either the bright sun or total darkness. The sun could be seen only if they looked at it directly. But they dared not risk this, fearing that the intensity would be great enough to blind them, and so they saw blackness continually.

In the beginning this darkness was fascinating. But after many days it became oppressive. Jack longed for an azure sky with white clouds scudding across it, the kind of sky he could see almost any morning from his bedroom window at home.

They were also oppressed by the vague feeling that time was standing still, that the *Lodestar* was not only suspended in space but also in time. On earth one knew that the day was over because the sun set and it became dark. When it became light again, a new day had dawned.

Not so in space. There was no rotation, no movement of the sun across the heavens, no day and no night. When they looked out of the ship they saw blackness. And whenever they looked out again, no matter if it were five minutes later or ten hours later, it was still black. So the crew lived by the clock. It was their only guide for telling them when to go to bed, when to arise, and when to do their various daily chores. The clock was a servant that helped them to maintain their routine.

One morning when Jack was awakening from a heavy sleep, he noticed through half-closed eyes that Dr. Shallot and Mr. Warick were acting in a strange manner. He rubbed his eyes to clear them and asked, "What are you doing? How come you're hanging onto those loops?"

As he spoke he started to unfasten the stabilizing belt that had been fastened around him when he went to sleep.

"We're approaching zero gravity, Jack," said Dr. Shallot. "Leave your belt fastened and stay right where you are."

Jack was anxious to get up; but Dr. Shallot continued to talk firmly. "We'll soon need these loop grips. When you release your belt, catch a grip and hang onto it. Even now it's difficult to move around because you have to push your foot down when you want to take a step. Hold on to a grip at all times. I don't expect anything unforeseen will happen, but it's best to be prepared."

"Golly," said Jack, his eyes popping, "I've been waiting for this." He was releasing his security belt and getting to his feet. "It's hard to believe all those things we've been talking about; but we'll soon know the answers."

"You mean about floating around in space?" asked Mr. Warick.

"Yes, that and liquids floating around in drops instead of pouring the way they should. I can't imagine how we could possibly float around in space. Why, it would be just like a goldfish lying still in the water."

Jack went to the food compartment and removed a saucepan.

"What are you going to do with that?" asked Don.

"Just this," answered Jack.

He dropped the saucepan and it fell to the floor, or rather, it floated to the floor. It did not fall abruptly with a bang as it would on earth where the gravity is great, but it went down slowly and settled on the floor of the compartment.

As Jack picked it up he said, "I'm going to keep dropping this until it doesn't drop any more."

"That won't be too long now, Jack," said Dr. Shallot. "We should be in the zero gravity zone in only a few minutes."

Jack went to his chair with difficulty. It was hard to walk, for the gravity was not great enough to pull his legs down quickly, and they had to be pushed down. He sat in the chair and dropped the pan, watched it float to the floor, then picked it up again. He did this over and over.

And then it did not fall. It hung in space.

"Look," he cried. He was too dumbfounded to say any more.

"Look, look at that," cried Mr. Warick with astonishment. "It's staying there just as if it were resting on a table."

Jack ran his hand under the pan.

"That's just about the silliest thing I ever saw," said Mr. Warick with disbelief. "It looks as though there were a ghost holding it there."

"Maybe it's Hank Sylvester who's doing it," said Dr. Shallot. "He may have been with us all the time."

In the excitement Jack reached for the pan with a sharp motion. This threw him out of his chair and he hung in space, completely helpless. He could not move himself in any direction at all. He flailed his arms about, but nothing happened. He moved his legs, kicking them as if he were swimming, but he was motionless. He did not settle toward the floor.

"I'm helpless," he said. "I can't move one bit."

"Reach out your hand," ordered Dr. Shallot, "and I'll try to get hold of it."

Jack stretched as far as he could, but could not touch Dr. Shallot's fingers.

"Hold on a moment," said Dr. Shallot as he moved to a nearer loop grip.

This time Jack could reach Dr. Shallot's hand, and he pulled Jack to him.

Jack expected to be disciplined for his foolishness in letting go of his grip. But Dr. Shallot was in no mood for scolding.

"Keep a tight hold of this grip, Jack. I'm going to try floating around."

He hopped a little and was suspended in air, just as Jack had been a moment before. There was little danger in his doing this for the floating member of the crew could be reached with ease in the confines of the small compartment.

Then Jack worked his way to the food compartment where he put a cup under the spout and caught some water as it was pushed out by the pressure behind it. With some apprehension he turned the cup upside down, half expecting the water to pour out of it in spite of what he had been told. But it didn't; the water stayed there, just as though it were fastened to the cup. Jack shook the cup but nothing happened. He shook it harder and the water came out, but not in a stream. It was in small round drops that went floating around the compartment like a mist.

A few minutes later both the droplets and the cup, which had been floating in space all this time, settled to the floor, and the crew knew they had entered into the gravitational field of Mars. The zero gravity zone existed at that place where the gravitational field of earth tapered down to nothing, and the gravity of Mars was of such a small degree that it was not effective.

Once they were within Mars' sphere of influence and in an area of increasing gravity, Dr. Shallot checked the speed of the *Lodestar* and found that there was a slight acceleration. This was expected, for the gravity of Mars was now pulling the ship toward it, whereas before the ship had been moving against the pull of gravity of earth.

He allowed the *Lodestar* to speed to a maximum of 30,000 miles an hour. The forward jets had been cut down for some time because the inertia of the ship was enough to keep it in motion. When maximum speed was reached, the reverse jets were brought into operation to prevent any further acceleration.

When Dr. Shallot checked the temperature gauge he found that it was steady. Although the temperature control mechanism was highly effective, the dull silver color of the ship also helped to prevent overheating. This color reflected the sunlight that fell upon it, and so kept the heat from building up. If it were darker in color, the skin would have become so hot that the refrigerating equipment would have been functioning continually and at top speed.

Several times each day Dr. Shallot switched on the radar equipment, and scanned the heavens as a routine matter. Once or twice during the journey small blips showed up on the screen, but most of the time it was a perfect blank. He now turned on the radar and looked at the screen.

As he peered, Mr. Warick said, "Do you see anything of Hank?"

Absent-mindedly the doctor grunted, "Humph, what's that?"

"I said, 'Do you see anything of Hank?' Do you see him on the scope?"

"Oh," said Dr. Shallot as he continued to look, "you mean Hank Sylvester. No, not a sign of him, or anything else for that matter."

Mr. Warick was in a reflective mood. He rested his chin on his thumb. "You know," he said, "that Hank must have been pretty slick."

"Oh, I don't know," said Jack. "He probably borrowed a gun to go hunting, and found the grass a lot greener on the other planet."

"And so he kept moving on and on," put in Mr. Warick.

Suddenly Dr. Shallot tensed. He raised his shoulders and turned them inward as he hunched forward to get a better view of the screen.

"This probably isn't Hank," he said, "but something peculiar is showing up here. Look!"

Mr. Warick and Jack craned their necks to get a better view. Small blips showed up every minute or so and then disappeared. Sometimes they started as pinpoints, grew until they were the size of marbles, and then were gone. At other times they were somewhat larger to begin with.

"I don't like it," said Dr. Shallot quietly and more to himself than to either Jack or Mr. Warick. He concentrated on the screen before him.

"Let's hope the blips don't get any larger," said Mr. Warick.

As they stared at the screen Jack remembered what

Mr. Warick had said about a collision. At 30,000 miles an hour it wouldn't take too large an object to smash the shiny rocket. It was senseless to say anything, so Jack kept quiet.

Dr. Shallot was glued to the scope. He was mumbling softly to himself and rubbing his left temple hard. He kept muttering, "Don't like it. Don't like it at all."

Mr. Warick and Jack were stretching so much to see the screen that their heads were almost touching. They were gasping short breaths, not daring to relax or inhale deeply.

Jack was watching a dot the size of a pinpoint somewhat to the left of the center of the scope. It grew larger constantly, until it was about as big as a golf ball. He expected it to disappear as had all the others; but this one grew larger and larger.

"Oh, no," he cried softly.

He swallowed nothing over and over again, and gripped the arms of his chair so hard that he burst a tiny blood vessel in his finger tip.

And the blip kept growing.

Dr. Shallot was calm. He showed no outward signs of the tension he must have felt, other than the determined rubbing of his left temple.

Not so with Mr. Warick. His eyes were opened so wide that they looked as though they might pop from his head.

Jack's stomach was tied in knots, and it felt as though it were filled with lead.

And the blip grew larger.

"Why don't we veer off," screamed through Jack's mind. "Why doesn't he kick in the side jets?"

And then Jack saw that Dr. Shallot was trying frantically to move them. He was pushing one button after another but there was no response. Something had jammed in the control panel.

This was doom coming at them. This was destiny. What a sorry way to end a heroic exploit. And what a horrible death it would be. The ship would be shattered, reduced to so many particles of rubble. The outward pressure in the bodies of the men was fifteen pounds on every square inch of surface. There would be no inward pressure, so they would be burst like so many toy balloons that had been filled with too much air.

And the blip kept growing.

Then, all in a moment, the screen was clear. There was not a single object showing.

They all exhaled deeply. They looked thankfully at one another. Words did not come easily.

Jack moaned, "Whew, that was close."

"Too doggoned close," said Mr. Warick.

Dr. Shallot had not relaxed. His hands were steady as he checked the radius of coverage of the screen. He found it was two degrees from dead ahead and so the obstacle or object that had been seen on the screen was never in the path of the ship. The screen had cleared quickly as it passed to port.

Mr. Warick scrambled over to the steering jet controls to throw a circuit breaker that had closed and locked them into position. Dr. Shallot and Jack kept their eyes glued to the scope. Suddenly another large blip was visible. It grew instantly, but there was no worrying about it. There was no time. Before they had a chance to prepare for it, the ship was thrown crazily off course as though some great giant had picked it up and hurled it.

Jack and Dr. Shallot, both of whom were fastened securely, spun around in their seats. Around and around they went.

The *Lodestar* was careening through space, looping, diving, and spinning like a powerful tarpon fighting the hook that is burning into its jaws.

Mr. Warick, who was out of his seat, grabbed at the walls, hoping that his hand would strike a nylon grip. He felt the loop and hung on with all his strength; but it was not enough. A quick dive of the ship, followed by an abrupt change of direction threw him into a faint and his grip loosened. He rolled about the compartment like a basketball on a seesaw.

Jack caught momentary glimpses of the instrument

panel. The dials were spinning around and around. Pointers slewed to the right and then to the left. Lights blinked incessantly. He felt a heavy weight against his shoulder. He reached for it and held on. Somehow he knew that it was Mr. Warick he was holding onto, so he tensed his body against the restraining belt and exerted his utmost strength.

Dr. Shallot went into unconsciousness and out again so many times that it was hard to know whether his actions were planned or instinctive. He groped for the power control that would throw the jets into full speed. But there was no finding it. When he was facing away from the panel he tried to swing himself about but the careening *Lodestar* threw him away. Gradually he was able to pull himself around and reach the lever. He gave the ship full power and the great force of the jets slowly overcame the hectic motions.

Jack continued to hold onto Mr. Warick who was slumped over him, limp as a bag of feed and twice as heavy.

Dr. Shallot was fighting the ship back to stability, working at it with a fervor and strain that could have been no greater had he been pushing the nose of the ship with his own bare hands.

Jack was groggy but he knew enough to slap Mr. Warick, rub his wrists, and jostle him in an effort to bring him to consciousness. As the *Lodestar* steadied, Jack slipped out of his belt and dragged Mr. Warick into the seat where he fastened him. Mr. Warick groaned softly.

"Mr. Warick," called Jack, "Don, can you hear me?"

There was no response at first, but gradually he became conscious.

Meanwhile Dr. Shallot was having some success in his efforts to right the ship. The dials and indicators were settling down to their normal position. He shut down the jets and was checking his course and velocity.

From the time of the impact not a word had been spoken. Now that the excitement was over, the crew had time to realize the peril they had been through. But their words were commonplace.

"Whew," said Mr. Warick, "I feel as though I just went a few rounds with a champion boxer, and got the worst of it."

"You certainly bounced around, Don."

"Do you suppose we hit a meteor, Doctor?" asked Jack.

"I don't think so, Jack. If we had hit one it would have finished us. I think we came close to a large one, though, and its gravitational field threw us off course."

This was exactly what had happened. If the *Lodestar* had hit a meteor, no matter how small, the impact would have been so great that the ship would have disintegrated. Coming close to an object large enough to have a con siderable magnetic field would disrupt the path of the ship. And yet the ship would not be drawn into the object because its inertia would be great enough to carry it beyond the field.

As all the equipment was fastened securely, the compartment was not in any great disorder, but this could not be said for the crew.

Mr. Warick grinned at them both. "The next time you start stunting, Doctor, give us a little warning. I wasn't at all ready that time. I didn't even have time to catch on to something."

Mr. Warick's good humor was just what was needed to ease the tension. But it was a long time before the crew calmed down completely. In fact, the next few hours were exciting beyond any they had ever lived, for they were approaching Mars.

7. THE LANDING

As THE DETAILS of earth faded into obscurity, and it became little more than a glowing spot in the heavens, the thoughts of the crew turned toward Mars, the red planet. As they approached closer to it, the crew felt a bond with their goal. They kept their eyes on it constantly as the details on the planet became more and more noticeable. At one point it had been only the size of a marble; then it had become as large as the moon, although it was much less bright. The light of the moon from the earth is yellow; but the light from Mars was an uneven brick red with darker and lighter areas here and there.

Jack was at the sight observing the planet. As he watched he said, "I hope the astronomers are right, and there is some air on Mars; but from here I don't see any signs of an atmosphere at all."

"Don't you see any clouds?" asked Dr. Shallot.

"Not a single one."

"Look at the edge of the planet, Jack," said the doctor. "While you're looking I'll swing the ship to starboard, and you keep your eye on the rim of the planet and the stars beyond it."

Jack kept his eye to the sight, and he saw the planet blot out the stars beyond it. They faded gradually, growing dimmer and dimmer.

"I see what you mean," said Jack. He turned toward Dr. Shallot who was bringing the *Lodestar* back on course. "The stars got dimmer because I was seeing them through an atmosphere. If there were no atmosphere they would have blanked out abruptly."

"That's it, Jack," agreed Dr. Shallot. "The planet has an atmosphere, but it's very thin compared to earth's."

Jack had turned back to the sight. After a moment or so, he spoke. "I guess the astronomers hit it right when they said there wasn't much water in the air, because there's not a single cloud."

"Maybe it's too early to know," cautioned Dr. Shallot. "When we get closer we may see clouds that are too thin to be visible from this distance."

"Perhaps you're right, Doctor." And then somewhat reflectively, he added, "I get wondering every once in a while, though."

"You mean if I'm right or not?"

"Oh, no, not that."

"You don't mean you're still wondering about the people on Mars?"

The possibility of the crew's finding living creatures on the planet had been an interesting topic of conversation on many occasions.

"I'm afraid so," answered Jack as he screwed up his face into one of its odd shapes. "I know the astronomers said there were none there at all. I respect them, but even they could be wrong. I still think there could be people there."

"Maybe so, maybe so," said Dr. Shallot as he rubbed his temple. And then he continued, "I haven't said much of this before, Jack, but I have some ideas about Mars and the life that might be there." It was true that he had done more listening than talking when the possibility of life on Mars was being discussed.

Jack leaned forward to pay closer attention as he continued. "I think *people* is the wrong word to use for the life on Mars, because I doubt if there are any human beings there. But I do expect there's some life. Not plant life, although I'm sure we'll find that, too; but animal life."

"But what kind of animal life, Doctor? Animal life could mean germs or insects, or maybe huge amoeba that sprawl themselves over the countryside like those dreamed up by H. G. Wells. They'd sure be cold, slithering things."

As Jack spoke, he frightened himself with the thought of meeting such creatures. "What would we do if we ever met things like that, great big insects or slimy jellied masses?"

"We have our rifles, Jack."

"I know, Dr. Shallot, but rifles wouldn't be any good against that sort of thing. Where would you shoot it, any-way?"

Dr. Shallot never did get a chance to tell Jack about the kind of animals he expected to find, for just then Mr. Warick, who had been napping, awoke.

"What are you two planning on shooting?" he asked sleepily.

"I was just wondering how we'd take care of any giant amoebas we might find on Mars," said Jack.

"That's easy," said Mr. Warick. "We'll just follow the plans we made before we left. First, try to make friends. If that doesn't work, use our rifles to scare them; and in the last event, use the rifles to protect ourselves." Mr. Warick stretched deeply. "But I wouldn't worry too much about that, Jack. The place is probably teeming with mild, pleasant, peace-loving creatures who will welcome us with open arms."

The thought appealed to Mr. Warick so he settled back in his seat and continued. "I can picture our reception. There will be a procession of natives bearing all sorts of exotic and succulent foods. We'll be seated at a table covered with a cloth of gold, with the king and queen and their beautiful daughters. As the natives pass by us with the trays of food, we'll select those that appeal to us. There'll be music and dancing and singing, and everyone will be madly happy. Oh, it'll be a glorious day."

"Go on and pipe dream," said Dr. Shallot. "To hear you talk one would think we were heading for the island of Bali, instead of for a planet where the temperature rarely goes above fifty degrees, and where it's probably a hundred below at night."

He continued, "No, Don, you paint a lovely picture, but I'm afraid you're too optimistic. And Jack's a pessimist. I think we're going to find something between the two extremes, no slithering creatures that will try to swallow us, but no land of milk and honey either."

"All I hope," said Jack, "is that whatever we find, there will be some appetizing food. I'm sure tired of eating dried meat and powdered potatoes."

Mr. Warick agreed quickly. "I'm tired of those concentrates, too. What I need is a good meal of fresh, juicy food. After that I want to stroll through wide open spaces. Being surrounded by nothing but emptiness is giving me the willies."

"I guess a change of scenery wouldn't hurt any of us," said Dr. Shallot.

He saw Jack yawn, and added, "Why don't you get a

few hours sleep, Jack. When you awaken we should be near enough to Mars to get a good look at it."

Jack rested for an hour or so. When he awakened, the *Lodestar* had moved much closer to Mars, and the men were discussing landing operations.

"What does she look like?" Jack asked of Mr. Warick who was at the sight.

"Take a look," he said as he turned away, "you're in for a surprise."

Jack moved to the peep sight, made a minor adjustment, and set his eye to it. What he saw made him speechless.

"What do you think of it?" asked Mr. Warick after Jack had been gazing for some time.

At first Jack had to shield his eyes from the intense light, for he had become used to seeing almost complete darkness through the sight, absolute darkness except for the stars. He now saw a brightness greater than the full harvest moon.

He was overwhelmed and answered simply, "It's beautiful, so colorful and cheerful looking."

Because the ship was within 350,000 miles of the planet, the view was remarkable. Mars seemed to be twice as large around as earth's moon appears from the earth. Since the sun was behind the ship, the entire planet was lighted brilliantly. The dominant color was a soft reddish orange with small green patches breaking its smoothness. The patches were dark at the center, and became less green and more orange away from the center. The planet was misted occasionally by a thin veil.

Here and there one could see splotches that were more intense than the reddish orange of the planet as a whole.

The north and south poles were covered with white. This was probably snow or frost, or perhaps solid carbon dioxide. But no matter what they were made of, these white caps were perfect accents for the other colors of the remarkably brilliant planet.

No white clouds were visible, although there was a brownish cloud of large proportions just north of the equator. This was apparently a dust storm that had been picked up by the planet's thin atmosphere. As the crew watched it, the cloud moved some distance from the spot where it was first noticed. This change of position strengthened the belief that it was a cloud of dust and not some disturbance peculiar to the planet.

"Why do you suppose the cap at the top of the planet is so much smaller than the one at the bottom?" asked Mr. Warick.

"Mars has a northern and a southern region and it has a change of seasons, just as earth does," explained Jack. "Right now the northern hemisphere is having spring and so the northern ice cap is melting and becoming smaller.

If you look closely you'll see a dark fringe around the cap. That's probably the water that has come from the melting snow."

It would be several hours before a landing could be made; but every one of the crew was tense and anxious to have it over in spite of—or perhaps because of—the dangers. Pulses were beating harder and stronger with every round of the clock, for the ship was moving close to its goal, a goal 35,000,000 miles from the starting point.

Mr. Warick was especially nervous. He passed some time by washing himself thoroughly, shaving, and combing his hair (what little there was of it). He then put on the brightest bow tie in his collection, a luxury which he still allowed himself.

"What's that for?" asked Jack as he looked at the tie.

Mr. Warick answered him as he straightened it. "Nothing like being prepared, I always say. In a few hours we may be meeting some very nice people, and I want them to know that I'm completely civilized."

"That tie wouldn't prove it," said Jack. "In fact, I think it would frighten anyone away, even if he wanted to be friendly."

Dr. Shallot turned to look at the tie. "How did you keep a prize like that hidden for so long, Don? I've never seen it before."

"Thank you, Doctor. The truth is that I've been saving it for the reception."

"You mean the reception with the king and queen, and the delicious foods?"

"Of course," said Mr. Warick. "We should look respectable for our first appearance."

But the men knew that they could not leave the ship as soon as they landed for the exhaust tube would have to cool, and it would have to be purified and made less radioactive, for it was now deadly. So there would be plenty of time to prepare for any reception. But Dr. Shallot entered into the spirit.

"You're right," he agreed. As he spoke he stroked his beard and mustache. From the time the voyage started, he had stopped shaving and his beard was now luxuriant.

"Maybe I ought to shave this off," he suggested.

"Don't think of it," said Mr. Warick. "Why, for all we know the Martians might think a beard is tremendously important."

Mr. Warick laughed as he spoke, and had a twinkle in his eye. But he did not realize the truth of his words.

Hours sped by while the crew took turns at the sight. Definite markings could be seen on the surface of Mars. These were probably what earth astronomers had assumed were canals. From the vantage point of the Lodestar, now within 100,000 miles of the planet, it was obvious that the markings were not canals, although it was still impossible to say just what they were. Aside from these lines and numerous darker spots scattered about the surface, the planet was smooth and fairly uniform in appearance. There seemed to be no hills or valleys, no plateaus or canyons, no forests or bodies of water.

The entire northern half of the planet, which was the only part that could be seen now that the *Lodestar* was so close, was cast in a reddish glow. The glow was broken now and then by small, dark spots and narrow lines, the greenish areas and the polar caps of clean white.

After Jack had been looking through the sight for several minutes, Mr. Warick asked, "Can you see Hank Sylvester?"

"No, I can't make him out yet," replied Jack. "But seriously, we're so close now that I believe we could pick out cities if there were any."

"Maybe so, Jack. But I doubt it, we're still a long distance away."

What Mr. Warick called a long distance, and what Jack called a long distance were two different things. As Jack looked through the sight, he could see only Mars. It seemed to him that the *Lodestar* was hurtling directly into the middle of the planet. As he gazed through the sight, this feeling became stronger. He was bewitched and held to the sight just as a pilot is sometimes bewitched into holding to a course which his senses tell him is wrong. Jack's heart was thumping as he said excitedly, "She looks mighty close."

Dr. Shallot, calm as always, moved to the sight.

"Yes, it seems close, Jack," he said, with no sign of disturbance in his voice. "We'll check with radar to get a fix."

He switched on the instrument and peered at the screen. A series of blips appeared instantly. By studying a cluster of dials, the doctor could determine the interval that elapsed between the time an impulse was sent out and its echo was received. From this interval he could compute the distance to the target. Mr. Warick and Jack peered over his shoulder as he made the readings.

"We're sixty-eight thousand miles from the planet," he announced. "We had better strap down loosely, and make other preparations for deceleration."

"Wow," Jack exclaimed, "this is it!"

The doctor smiled. "Don't get all worked up, Jack. It'll be two and a half hours before we set down."

Mr. Warick went to the sight for a last look. He could see little more than a vast dull redness sloping off at the horizon, indicating the planet's curvature.

He moved over to his seat and strapped down. Jack and Dr. Shallot did likewise. Without being aware of it, each of them was becoming tense. This was a nerve-racking time, for the slightest error in judgment could swamp the ship. No one had ever landed a rocket of this type; and, although test after test had been made with models, no one knew that every possibility of error had been eliminated. And there was anxiety about the terrain of Mars. Although it looked solid and therefore safe, there was no way of knowing whether this was so, or whether it was semiliquid and would swallow the *Lodestar* as the ocean gulps a sinking liner.

Dr. Shallot looked at Jack and Mr. Warick. "Ready to decelerate?" he asked.

"Ready, Doctor."

"Ready."

"We'll step up the reverse jets to full power," he announced as he reached high above him and pulled a recessed lever.

The ship had been hurtling onward, accelerating as it was pulled by the gravity of Mars. Before it could be maneuvered into a landing, its velocity had to be cut down.

In a few minutes the crew were thrown forward against the restraining belts as the forward jets went into action and slowed the *Lodestar*. Jack's head felt heavy, and there was a great pressure on his ribs, but these sensations diminished rapidly as his body adjusted itself to the changed velocity. The deceleration continued for twenty minutes. Dr. Shallot looked steadily at the radar screen while Jack and Mr. Warick watched the dials that indicated the temperature of the ship itself, and also the distance indicator, which had been set on automatic.

"Fifty thousand miles," announced Mr. Warick. He and Jack continued to stare at the meter.

"Forty-nine thousand miles," called out Mr. Warick. And this continued until he called 40,000 miles.

Dr. Shallot reached above his head and pushed the lever that shut off the forward jets. Then he pushed two red buttons in a square of four. These operated the two steering jets on the port side of the ship. The action of these jets threw the nose of the *Lodestar* to starboard. As the ship swerved, a terrific force caused by their own inertia threw the crew to the left. The ship was straining to go in a straight line but the two powerful steering jets were forcing it to change direction slowly. The *Lodestar* was moving in toward Mars rapidly, no longer in a perpendicular line, but at an angle. Closer and closer it moved, the steering jets still operating at full power. When it was within five thousand miles of the planet, the *Lodestar* leveled off and was moving in a path parallel to the surface of Mars.

"So far so good," said Dr. Shallot without taking his eyes from the controls. "Now comes the big test."

He reached for the control rod that operated the main jets. With a determined motion he moved the lever to full on. The ship quivered like a horse about to leap forward, and then lunged ahead with its nose turning away from the planet and heading out into space just as though it had taken off from Mars itself.

Jack could feel the blood draining from his head and piling up in his stomach. He leaned over as far as his restraining belt would let him, fighting the nausea that was becoming unbearable. He recovered enough to turn his head so he could see Dr. Shallot and Mr. Warick, both of whom were in similar positions. Now there was no fear in their hearts. Just as a soldier loses all fear of death once he engages in battle, the crew forgot their dread, so great was their physical anguish and excitement.

The *Lodestar* continued to turn until it was perpendicular to Mars with its nose pointing into the heavens. The steering jets were shut off completely, and the power in the main jet was decreased so that the ship was motionless, standing in space on its tail, holding a position where the force of its jet equalized the gravitational pull of the planet.

Doctor Shallot had recovered from his nausea and was acting as though he were alone in the ship, so intent was he on the job before him. He threw a series of click switches that were controls for the automatic landing device, and pushed all four buttons for the steering jets, although these did not function immediately. And then he relaxed, for there was little else for him to do. The automatic lander was a complex pilot device that kept the ship stable through the action of dual gyroscopes. If the *Lodestar* veered from its perpendicular position, the steering jets would bring it back.

There was also a radio altimeter that kept a constant check on the distance between the ship and the planet. This information operated controls that reduced the force of the jets enough to allow the *Lodestar* to settle slowly. At first the ship came down rapidly, but as the distance became less it lowered more and more slowly.

Jack, Mr. Warick, and Dr. Shallot said nothing, for they were too concerned with the instruments they were watching. Their heads were thrown back so they could stare at the instrument panel which was now overhead because of the changed attitude of the ship. They were strapped securely in their seats and so were hampered in their movements. The position they had to assume in order to see the dials was most uncomfortable.

Mr. Warick bent his head forward and turned it from left to right to get the kinks out of his neck. Still there was silence. Each of them was too busy thinking, hoping, and supposing to take time to talk. They were supposing many things.

Suppose the automatic pilot should go awry. The *Lodestar* would fall onto its side and continue falling over for there would be no way to stop the motion. It would head straight into Mars to bury its shiny nose in the terrain.

Or suppose the surface of the planet should be an ooze that would swallow the *Lodestar* along with her crew.

Or suppose the ship were surrounded by hostile creatures that would swarm over it and destroy it before the men could get outside.

Thoughts like these raced through their heads, each new one chasing out the old one as they sometimes do in a bad dream.

All eyes turned to the radio altimeter. It was slipping below the hundred-foot mark. Ninety feet registered on the dial, and then fifty, twenty-five, and ten.

When the altimeter hit ten feet, Dr. Shallot ordered, "Throw the stilt control."

Jack's hand had been on the knob of the control for so long waiting for this order that his arm was almost asleep. But this was the word he had been waiting for and he did not hesitate. He threw the control to the right strongly. As he did so, three legs like those of a tripod telescoped out of the ship, emerging from a point about one-third above the tail.

The altimeter was hovering at zero. Slowly but steadily it crept to the left, showing that the *Lodestar* was inching closer to the surface. It hit zero. An instant later three green lights shone brilliantly on the instrument panel.

These sparkling lights showed that each of the three legs had made contact with something solid.

"We made it," cried Jack. "We're in!"

The men stared at the green lights, which glowed steadily without a single flicker.

There was a moment of dead silence when soundless words of thanksgiving were said by each man to himself and then, unable to restrain themselves, each one of them burst with congratulations.

"We've done it, we've done it," cried Mr. Warick.

Dr. Shallot's eyes sparkled, showing the pride he felt. He threw all the controls to off, except for the steering jets. These were kept idling so that the ship could be stabilized, should it begin to settle. He reached to both Jack and Mr. Warick and shook each man's hand in turn, covering the hand affectionately with his left.

"Men," he said, "I congratulate you." There was thankfulness in his voice. "We've reached another planet, something that's been dreamed about for thousands of years."

The splendor of the moment quickened the pulses of all three men and made their eyes glisten with tears. Each had the greatest respect and admiration for the others.

Mr. Warick broke the spell. "Well," he said huskily as he reached to undo his restraining belts, "let's see what kind of a place we've come to. It looked barren from away up there. Perhaps it'll look better close up."

WHEN JACK looked through the sight he was blasted by light—bright, intense, and blinding. It was startling and made him squint his eyes tightly. For weeks he had been looking through the sight and had seen little more than utter darkness. As his eyes became adjusted to the brightness he saw the surface of the planet. It was dull red, and rolled softly for miles and miles with not a single hill, mountain, or tree to break the straight horizon line. The reddish color of the ground predominated, and at first Jack thought that the entire surface was red. But as he looked closer he could see darker areas which appeared to have a greenish cast. When he looked at the ground near the ship, however, he thought he saw stones of various sizes, but of this he could not be sure because there was some distance between the sight and the ground.

"Golly," said Jack with discouragement, "it looks just

like a desert out there. I don't see how anything could live on it."

"It certainly doesn't look very inviting," agreed Dr. Shallot. "But there's more to the planet than the part we can see. We'll do some exploring as soon as we can go through the jet tube. Maybe we'll find an area that's more fertile looking."

Mr. Warick was at the sight, and speaking as he observed. "The sun is getting low in the sky. Our exploring will have to wait until tomorrow because the sun will set before too long."

"I'm afraid you're right, Don," said Dr. Shallot. "It's too bad that we have to wait that long, but we'd better not leave the ship while it's dark."

No one slept well that night. They were excited at the thought of setting foot on a planet that had never been trod by man. And they were restless, for there was the constant possibility of an attack by some sort of Martian creature. The *Lodestar* was alert throughout the night, for one of the men was always on watch, and the steering jets were kept idling in case they had to take off quickly.

When the sun rose it found the crew out of bed and breakfasted. The temperature of the jet tube had dropped to one hundred fifty degrees, so the temperature was low enough for the men to pass through. But it had to be freed of harmful radiation. Dr. Shallot opened a valve which released a heavy gas that acted as a radiation purifier. This fell slowly through the tube and rinsed it of harmful radioactive particles, rendering it safe for the passage.

Jack climbed into the nose section of the ship to get the suits that the men would wear when they left the ship. He handed them down to Mr. Warick.

"I guess you have all of them, Mr. Warick," he said after he had handed down numerous bundles.

"I think so, Jack. Come on down and we'll check them over."

The suits were called pressure suits, although a better name might have been pressure-equalizing suits. The pressure inside the suits was kept at a steady fifteen pounds per square inch, which is the pressure most comfortable for the body, no matter how low the outside pressure might become. The suit covered the body entirely; hands and feet as well as arms, legs, torso, and head. If this were not done, the pressure inside the body would be so much greater than the pressure pushing inward that the men would burst like a balloon.

The basic material used throughout the suits was plastic, which was stronger than metal of equal weight, but much lighter. The plastic was impregnated with an alloy that was able to reflect ultraviolet light and cosmic rays. If one were to be exposed to these radiations, he would be killed in a very few minutes. On earth the atmosphere was thick enough to filter out most of these rays; but on Mars the air was so thin that the crew expected the rays to come through.

The arms from the shoulder down, and the legs from the hip down were built in movable sections that gave them a corrugated appearance. The sections enabled the wearer to move freely. The feet and torso were made of a less flexible material, but even these parts could move to a limited extent.

The entire head was covered with a large, clear plastic globe that looked exactly like an inverted fish bowl. Before putting on this globe the men donned close-fitting khaki helmets. These served not only to keep their hair out of their eyes, but also as a further precaution against harmful radiations, since the material was treated with reflecting alloys.

Their hands were covered with glovelike devices which seemed clumsy, but were not. They could manipulate each finger with ease, and could reach a high degree of accuracy and facility with only a little practice.

Even when their bodies were completely covered by these suits, the men were able to move about in them quite freely. The suits weighed only thirty pounds earth weight, complete with equipment. Since the gravity of Mars was only a little more than one third that of earth, this weight became only one third as much, or about ten pounds, so the suit was not much of a burden.

The equipment in the suit consisted of a built-in radio receiver and sender, enabling them to converse even when they were completely covered and far removed from each other.

Two long tubes were connected to each of the suits, and ran to pressure-temperature regulators in the rocket. Air of the proper temperature (between 65 and 75 degrees), pressure, and composition (80 per cent nitrogen and 20 per cent oxygen) was kept moving through the tubes. The temperature of the air could be moved up or down rapidly if they encountered unusually cold or warm areas.

The possibility that the air hoses might be cut was anticipated, as well as the possibility that the crew might want to go into an area where they could not drag the hoses. To meet such an emergency, each suit contained an auxiliary tank of compressed air. If the hoses were detached, the valves attached to the suits were closed and the auxiliaries switched on. The air in these would sustain a man forty-five minutes, or one hour if he used a minimum amount of exertion.

Each suit was equipped with a small storage battery that supplied current to a transparent conducting material embedded between the layers of the head globe.

This current kept the globe warm and thus reduced the possibility of condensation of water vapor and clouding, a condition that would have occurred when the auxiliary air supply was being used. The current from the battery also supplied power to heating wires built into the plastic. These could keep the wearer warm for an hour and ten minutes.

Small packs of silica gel, which is able to take in large amounts of water, were placed inside the globes to absorb the water vapor in exhaled breath. Otherwise the air within the suits and globes would have become saturated rapidly, making it nauseating and unbearable.

As Mr. Warick and Jack were moving the pressure suits out of the nose section, Dr. Shallot was peering through the sight.

Suddenly he exclaimed excitedly, "Jack, Don, look here. There's something sparkling out there, I'm sure."

Jack and Don scrambled to the sight and they too could see a sparkling object in the distance. Distances were deceiving, as they learned later, but it looked as though the object was about a mile away.

The sparkle seemed to be caused by something that was moving in such a manner that it caught the sun occasionally and reflected light to the ship.

"There must be something alive out there," exclaimed Jack. "First you see the light and then you don't."

"It certainly seems so, Jack. But it could be something moved by the air."

"Let's get out there," exclaimed Jack. "Two months cooped up in here is long enough. I can't wait to set foot on good solid earth."

"Solid Mars would be better, Jack," said Mr. Warick. "Don't forget where you are."

"Jack is right," agreed Dr. Shallot. "Two months is long enough. Let's get on these suits and move outside." Then Mr. Warick spoke slowly. "I think that one of us had better remain in the ship. The pressure pump may not work right, or something else may go wrong. Someone will have to be here to check everything. After we've been out a few times, and learn our way about, we can be more carefree. Now we should take every precaution."

"Right you are," agreed Dr. Shallot. "Let's toss up to see who'll remain aboard."

"No need for that," said Mr. Warick. "I'll stay aboard."

"Not at all," put in Jack. "Since I'm the youngest, I'm the one who should stay in the ship."

It was hard for Jack to say this for he was straining to set foot on Mars. But he had long ago learned that a gentleman always puts the desires of others before his own.

Dr. Shallot would not listen to this. "No, I won't have it that way," he said. "We'll toss. It's the only fair way."

Although Jack and Mr. Warick argued, a coin was tossed and Dr. Shallot won. The coin was tossed again to decide between Jack and Mr. Warick, and Jack won. So Dr. Shallot and Jack were to make the first exploration and Mr. Warick would remain aboard the *Lodestar*.

Mr. Warick helped both of them into their suits. Whenever Jack saw anyone in these suits, he always thought of an ogre or some other sinister being. It never ceased to amuse him to see kindly Dr. Shallot in the weird-looking contraption. And Jack looked just as funny to Dr. Shallot.

When they were in the suits, they connected temporary air hoses. They then sat for five minutes inside the ship to become accustomed to the atmospheric conditions within the suits, and to check the apparatus.

The controls for the radios were encased in a small box fastened to the waist. Mr. Warick could hear whatever either of the men said, and he could speak to both of them.

After five minutes had elapsed the great adventure started. Small valves leading into the doctor's suit were closed until he left the ship and connected the outer hoses. Mr. Warick noted a small red light on the instrument panel which indicated that the outer door of the escape hatch was closed. He rolled back a small section of the foam-rubber lining to disclose the panel through which the crew had entered the ship. This he moved aside and Dr. Shallot wriggled through. As he was entering the hatch Jack could overhear the conversation between Dr. Shallot and Mr. Warick.

"Good luck, sir," said Mr. Warick. "Keep talking the first few minutes so I can be sure you are all right."

"Righto, Don. I'm sorry you're not going out, too."

"Forget it, Doctor. I'll make it next time."

Then he added, "Keep an eye peeled for Hank. He may have beat us here after all."

As the panel was closing over the doctor's head, Jack bade him good luck and assured him that he would be right behind him.

The next sound that Jack heard was Dr. Shallot's voice coming over the receiver within his head globe.

"I'm about to open the panel that leads outside," he said. "I have the handle, I'm—"

There was a heavy grunt, a thud, and then silence. Jack stared at Mr. Warick. He was frightened.

"Dr. Shallot," called Mr. Warick frantically into the microphone, "are you all right?"

Over and over again he shouted but the only response was silence, as deep as a tomb. He dared not open the hatch for he could not be sure the outer door was completely closed. If it were not, the air in the ship would rush out and carry everything in the ship with it, including the crew.

But even while Mr. Warick was speaking, Dr. Shallot's voice came through. "Hello, hello, there," he called. "I guess I was dazed for a few moments."

"You sure were," said Jack. "Are you all right?"

"Yes, yes. Everything is all right."

"What happened to you?"

"I should have known better. When I opened the outer panel, I was knocked against it as the air in the chamber rushed out. The vacuum is terrific. When you open the outer door, brace yourself solidly and hold on. The strain will be tremendous; but hold on tightly, for it is over in a moment."

"I'll remember," Jack assured him. "Are you quite sure you're all right?"

"Yes, yes," he said impatiently. "I'm going ahead now. I'm lowering myself."

After a minute he continued, "Haven't hit the ground yet. There, there, I seem to have it now. It feels solid enough. I began to wonder because I sank through several inches of a dustlike layer before I hit it."

Jack looked at Mr. Warick. His face registered the closest attention as he followed every little sound that came over the speaker. Dr. Shallot was coming through again.

"The outer panel is closed. I'm connecting the pressure hoses." After a moment or so, he added, "All set. I'll stand next to the ship until you come out, Jack. Good luck to you, and remember to brace yourself."

Jack's heart was pounding like a trip hammer as Mr. Warick disconnected the hoses and closed the valves of his suit. He saw Don's mouth form the words "Are you okay?" but he could not hear because Mr. Warick had put down his microphone while helping Jack make ready. Jack nodded his head.

Mr. Warick handed him a revolver and then picked up the microphone to speak into it. "You'd better take this along. But I hope you won't need it."

"I hope not," Jack replied, "but I'll feel better knowing we have some protection. I sure wish you were going in my place, Mr. Warick."

"Forget it," he said. "You won fair and square, and I'll get out later in the day."

Dr. Shallot's voice broke in, "Everything all right in there? I'm waiting?"

"Be right with you," said Jack.

Mr. Warick clipped a leather pouch to a heavy equipment belt around Jack's waist. The pouch was to be used for specimens they would collect. He then slipped back the inner panel. Jack moved into the compartment and the door closed behind him.

Although the hatch was lighted, Jack had a feeling of complete loneliness when he entered it, as though he were sealed in a tin can. He was now hemmed in so closely that he could hardly move. It was a great effort to reach forward and open the door. He opened it ever so slightly. As he did so there was a great swoosh as the air within the compartment rushed out into the vacuumlike atmosphere of Mars. Fortunately Dr. Shallot had warned him about the great suction and, even though he was well braced, he used all his strength to keep from being thrown down sharply.

Once the initial shock was over there was no further strain. He threw back the outer door and let himself down slowly onto Mars. His feet swung about, brushing through the loose surface, searching for a footing.

"Welcome to Mars, Jack." Dr. Shallot sounded like a native greeting a stranger. "We'd better hook you up before we do anything else."

Jack moved toward the exterior hose connection, and Dr. Shallot made the couplings and then opened the valves. Now they were both free to move about.

"Jack," said the doctor, "we're the first earth men to set foot on Mars, perhaps the first men of any sort. An eerie feeling, isn't it?"

"Eerie is right," answered Jack. "I'm goose pimples all over. But I can't help feeling that men lived here at some time. Of course there aren't any here now, you can see that, but we may find some remains of them. That sparkle might be a clue."

"Maybe so," replied Dr. Shallot. And then he called to Mr. Warick. "We are safely out, and all connected."

"Fine," he answered. "What is it like out there?"

"The light is wonderful. It's a grand feeling to be surrounded by it again, even though it's not the same as the light on earth. The sky is a much deeper blue. It's so deep I see stars here and there. It's a strange feeling to be the only things alive on such a vast place."

"It must be," answered Mr. Warick. "What's the land like?"

"There aren't any rocks at all. All we see is red powder. It looks as though every rock that ever existed here has been worn down to dust. The dust is caked here and there so it looks like rocks; but it crumbles easily."

The two of them scuffed through the red powder, hoping to uncover some clue to the history of Mars, but they struck nothing. Then Dr. Shallot saw a darker area off to their right.

"We're going toward a dark patch, Don."

"What is it?" asked Mr. Warick.

"We can't tell yet. Let you know as soon as we can."

Jack was in the lead, moving rapidly toward the area.

"Careful, Jack," cautioned Dr. Shallot. "Don't hurry

until we're sure of the terrain. There might be a swamp under us or a pit. Take it easy."

Jack pulled up short. As they neared the darker area they could see that it was made of a reddish-green growth.

"Well," said Jack triumphantly, "we know there's plant life on the planet. Sort of looks like seaweed, doesn't it?"

"Yes, or some kind of moss."

As he spoke, Dr. Shallot leaned over, took a handful of the stuff and placed it in the specimen bag.

Mr. Warick, who could hear the conversation broke in. "That sounds good to me," he said. "But you'd better not move too far away from the ship."

"Right, Don. We're moving back right now."

Jack was disappointed, for he wanted to strike out toward the sparkle they had seen. But he knew that the exertion would be too tiring. Their exercise aboard the *Lodestar* had been limited and they would have to tone up their muscles before they could walk any distance.

"What about that sparkle out there, Doctor. Are we going to investigate it?"

"We certainly are, Jack, but we can't take chances by going there now. In a day or so we'll be stronger, and we'll set out for it then."

He was walking at Jack's left. Abruptly he stopped and called, "Come over here, Jack. What do you make of this?"

He was brushing aside the powder with his foot, laying bare an area about a foot square.

"What are you doing?" asked Jack. But even as he asked, he could see that Dr. Shallot had unearthed something. He helped brush away the powder, and soon they could see a piece of fabricated metal. It looked somewhat like a gear and a shaft. It was weathered and pitted over most of its surface and looked as though it had lain there for many years.

"What are you doing out there?" asked Mr. Warick.

"We've found a piece of metal, Don," said the doctor excitedly, "and it looks very much like part of a machine."

"Jack," continued Dr. Shallot in the same excited voice, "this means there have been civilized beings here. Creatures who were intelligent enough to make a machine."

"Golly, Dr. Shallot, if we can find something like this right under our noses, we ought to find a lot more if we look farther."

"Right you are. But we'd better get back into the *Lodestar* now. We've been out long enough. Even a few minutes is tiring."

They moved back toward the escape hatch of the ship. When they arrived, Dr. Shallot radioed Mr. Warick to place thermometers and gas-collecting tubes in the perforated can in the hatch.

This can was a bucket-type holder that was full of holes, like a strainer or colander. The thermometers were placed in the bucket and the bucket was then hooked to the wall of the hatch, the inner door of which was then closed. When the outer door was opened, the air rushed out. The thermometers would have been pushed out by the air if they were not in the perforated bucket. In fact, the bucket itself would have been pushed out if it were not fastened to the wall.

When the thermometer was placed in direct sunlight it registered 50 degrees. The *Lodestar* landed at a point slightly north of the equator. If the temperature was only 50 degrees here, it must have been much colder in the polar regions, and in those regions comparable to the earth's temperate zones.

A maximum-minimum thermometer was left outside the ship. This was a device which indicated the highest and lowest temperatures reached during any period of time. When readings were made later, the doctor found that the lowest temperature reached during the night was 108 degrees below zero, which is the temperature of dry ice. The air was so thin that it was unable to prevent the escape of heat from the planet and it cooled down rapidly when the sun was no longer shining upon it.

Dr. Shallot opened six gas-collecting tubes, closed them

with stoppers and then placed them inside the leather pouch.

"I think we're ready to enter the ship, Jack. Are you all set?"

"Yes sir, Dr. Shallot, all ready."

"We're coming in, Don. Is the panel closed?"

"All closed. Hurry up so I can see what you found."

"In you go, then, Jack."

Jack raised himself into the hatch and closed the outside door. Once more that feeling of utter loneliness overcame him. He opened the inner door slowly. As he did, air from inside the ship rushed into the compartment with crushing force. He was dizzy from the shock, but the feeling passed quickly. Mr. Warick opened the panel far enough for Jack to pass through, and helped him into the ship. He was glad to be in familiar surroundings again.

Mr. Warick closed the inner panel immediately and directed Dr. Shallot to come in.

Soon the two of them had removed their suits and were discussing their impressions.

Dr. Shallot and the other two looked over the mosslike material, surface dust, and other materials that had been gathered. In some ways the moss looked like seaweed, and in some ways it was more like the lichens that grow in the arctic regions of earth. It was unlike any plant any of them had ever seen.

"No matter what it is," said Mr. Warick, "whether it is a moss or a lichen or something else, it is a plant, and it proves that there is life on the planet. That's the important thing."

"It sure does that," agreed Jack. "And if there's plant life, then there may be animal life, because it's hard to imagine how one can exist without the other."

Another thought occurred to Jack. "I wonder if all the green patches we saw when we were coming in to land are made of this same stuff."

"I don't see any reason why they should be," said Mr. Warick. "After all we have different plants all over the earth. Some places have rubber trees, others have apple trees, some have corn, others rice. I don't see why it should be any different here."

"That sounds reasonable enough, Don," said Dr. Shallot. "I imagine this is a tropical growth, and that there are other kinds of growth in colder places."

"If the tropics produce only spindly moss like this," said Jack, "the growth farther north must be terribly sparse."

"Yes, it probably is."

"I expected that we would find moss, Doctor," said Mr. Warick, "but this iron gear is a complete surprise." As Mr. Warick examined the iron with great care, he continued speaking. "It's extremely well made," he said to

Jack. "Look here." He pointed out a particularly smooth section. "See how well machined it is, how precise and accurate it must have been when new. It took a high intelligence to make this. You can be sure of that."

"But it must have been made a long time ago," said Jack.

"It probably was," agreed the doctor. "I only hope we can find more signs of civilization. I'm beginning to think that this is our best hope, for now that I see the planet, I feel more strongly than ever that there aren't any creatures living here now."

"I admit we haven't had my formal reception yet," said Mr. Warick, "but I'm not at all convinced there aren't animals of some sort here. I still think we might find some."

"If we do find any," Jack said, "I sure hope they're friendly. And I wouldn't mind a bit if they had some juicy fresh meat and vegetables that they couldn't use."

The *Lodestar* was equipped with a compact laboratory. Mr. Warick prepared to make an analysis of the red powder. Jack let some of it trickle through his fingers. It felt to him like coarse cornstarch, with a flaky particle here and there.

After Mr. Warick had been working for some time, Jack asked, "Do you have any idea yet what it is?"

"It seems to be an oxide, Jack. And unless I'm mistaken we'll find different concentrations at different locations on the planet. I can't tell what else is in it besides oxygen; sometimes it looks like iron, and at other times it seems to be mercury. Can't tell precisely with this equipment."

"Maybe it's a combination of substances, a good many different things mixed together."

"Yes, I think that's it. At any rate it's safe. We can walk through it without harm."

"What do you mean, Mr. Warick? Did you think it would hurt us?"

"I wasn't sure. I wanted to make sure it contained nothing corrosive or irritating."

While Mr. Warick and Jack were talking, Dr. Shallot was taking photographs through the peep sight, and making a sketch of the surface of Mars. These would be placed in the log book of the *Lodestar,* in which all events were recorded in great detail.

He spoke as he turned from the sight. "Let's test those gases we collected, Don. We may find some of them useful, especially if there's oxygen. We can use all of that we can get hold of."

"Right you are, Doctor."

Mr. Warick picked up one of the gas-collecting tubes. They were actually nothing more than large test tubes. He placed the tube in a clamp and then ran a hollow needle through the stopper and into the tube. The needle was connected to glass tubing which in turn was fastened to a manual vacuum pump, and then to a series of analytical devices.

Jack felt like a sixth finger while Mr. Warick was doing this work, for there was nothing he could do to help. He was fascinated with the color reactions which took place, as well as the skill with which Mr. Warick handled the apparatus.

"I'm afraid there's not much oxygen here. Only about one one-thousandth as much as there is on earth."

"Humph," Jack grunted as he made a grimace, "I guess that means we'll have to get along on our own limited supply."

"I'm afraid so," agreed Mr. Warick reluctantly.

"There doesn't seem to be any carbon dioxide either. At least not enough to make any change in this limewater."

"There must be some," said Jack, "because the mosses need it in order to live."

"Well," said Mr. Warick, "let's leave a sample of the air in this flask. Maybe a reaction will show up later on."

Dr. Shallot was listening to the conversation. He broke in. "If there is very little oxygen and carbon dioxide, then what is the atmosphere made of?"

"I suspect it's nitrogen, Dr. Shallot. I'm running a test on it right now."

"Let's hope it is," said Dr. Shallot, "and not methane or ammonia, or some other poisonous gas. Nitrogen may not help us particularly; but it won't hurt us either."

"We're in luck, Doctor. It's nitrogen all right. The way I figure it, about 98 per cent. The rest is probably oxygen, carbon dioxide, and water vapor. I'd say it's a very nice atmosphere, very nice indeed."

During the afternoon Dr. Shallot and Mr. Warick went out, while Jack remained in the ship to check the controls.

Jack was sure that people had once lived on Mars. That night his mind was full of visions of them, of their homes and public buildings, their cities and the machines and tools they worked with. Sleep was slow to come for he was greatly excited. Dr. Shallot had promised to investigate the sparkle the next day, and Jack couldn't wait to start.

Everyone was up early the next morning. After eating a large breakfast they put on their pressure suits, and Mr. Warick and Dr. Shallot went outside the ship to test the auxiliary air tanks and make sure they would function properly. The battery-operated heating equipment was also tested. It was essential to have everything functioning properly once the hoses were uncoupled and they moved away from the *Lodestar*. All the tests were favorable so Jack joined the others outside the ship. In addition to the regular equipment, they carried a rifle with them and a strong, light rope. Snaps were fastened to the rope at intervals, and these snaps were fastened to loops in each man's equipment belt. In this way the crew were fastened together, much as mountain climbers are, so if anyone should step into a trap, a hidden pit, or some other accident should befall, each could help the other.

The sun had been up only a few minutes, but the atmosphere was already warm as they started to move toward the sparkle. It looked more like a bright spot on the landscape, a whitish area in a dull background, than like a jewel. Walking through the powder was easy, like scuffing through light, powdery snow. Every step was taken cautiously, however, and the ground was tested before a man's full weight was put upon his foot. Mr. Warick was in the lead, Jack was next, and Dr. Shallot brought up the rear.

They were still able to converse, even though they were not hooked up to the *Lodestar*. Their radios were self-contained, operating as they did on batteries, and needed no outside source of power.

"Let's move a bit faster, Don," Dr. Shallot suggested. "Remember, our oxygen supply is limited."

Mr. Warick quickened his pace as much as caution would allow. As they walked ahead each one strained his eyes to get a better view of the bright object.

"It looks like a chunk of glass to me," said Mr. Warick.

"Maybe it's a relic of some sort, or the remains of a statue," said Jack.

"Maybe it's a big cake of ice," suggested Mr. Warick.

"It couldn't be that," said Dr. Shallot as they hurried along. "It's not cold enough for ice to last. It would melt."

"Look, look, it's moving!" cried Jack loudly.

"Don't yell like that, Jack. You make my ears ring."

"Sorry," said Jack less loudly. "But look at it, it's moving. I can see it."

"It doesn't seem to me to be moving," said Mr. Warick. He continued to stare at it and then exclaimed loudly, "It *is* moving. Watch that thing go. It's turning like a huge lens scanning the sky."

As he spoke Mr. Warick moved closer to the glass. He was now within three hundred feet of it and could see it clearly.

Dr. Shallot warned him, "Don't move too close, Don. We don't know what the thing is, or what it might do."

Mr. Warick moved in cautiously. Dr. Shallot and Jack followed him, and before them was the strangest sight man had ever seen.

The sparkling object was unquestionably a lens, and stretched out for a quarter of a mile on either side of it was a wide arc of similar, but smaller lenses. They were mounted in a long shallow pit, and every one of them was turned to the same angle. The large lens seemed to serve as a master control that regulated the motion of all the others. No mechanism was visible; but, as the crew watched, the entire bank of glasses moved noticeably. About a mile beyond they saw another sparkling object, and far beyond that another one. Row upon row of these lens banks stretched as far as their eyes could see.

Jack moved closer to the main lens and leaned over it, trying to peer through it to see what made it move. As he did, a blast of air struck him in the face, causing him to stagger back like a man who has been shot. He lost his balance and fell flat on his back, burying himself in the red powder.

"Jack, Jack," shouted Dr. Shallot as he and Mr. Warick ran forward, "what hit you?"

As Mr. Warick lifted Jack, he continued to fire questions at him.

When the boy got back his breath he answered. "I don't know what happened. I leaned over the lens, didn't touch a thing I'm sure, and all of a sudden a blast of air hit me square in the face."

Mr. Warick was relieved. "Maybe Hank Sylvester's down there playing tricks on you?" he suggested.

"Jack," exclaimed Dr. Shallot, "if a blast of air hit you, there must be creatures of some sort who are here with us. That blast of air meant something, and I have an idea what."

As he spoke he picked up a handful of the red powder and threw it at the lenses. As soon as it fell on the glass, air jets blew it away in a cloud.

"Yes sir," he said, "that's what I thought would happen. When a lens is clouded with dust or anything else, air blows over it to clear it away. When you leaned over,

Jack, your shadow fell on a lens, and the jets let go to clear the darkened areas."

"That's it, Doctor," said Mr. Warick excitedly, "there are people under the ground and they're using solar energy to keep alive. These lenses probably concentrate the rays of the sun to produce heat in the same way I used to make enough heat to start fires with a burning glass when I was a youngster."

"You're right," said Jack, "and I'll bet they're people who aren't much different from us."

"Go ahead, you two, with your wild imaginings," said Dr. Shallot. "There may be creatures of some sort around here, but I still can't conceive how real people as we know them could live here, or down there either. For one thing, how could they grow their food? Or maybe you think they eat mineral foods, and don't have to grow any meat and vegetables?"

"I'd like to find out," Jack said. "If they do have fresh food it would be worth an awful lot to me to get hold of some."

"Forget it, Jack," said Mr. Warick. "Don't torture yourself by thinking about food. Let's move along this installation, and look it over. I'd like to see if there is a break somewhere, an entrance or exit door. I'm convinced that this is the top to an underground network, and I'll bet a plug nickel there are people living beneath us."

They moved along the lens bank warily. Step by step and foot by foot they covered the entire right segment but there was no opening, no break of any kind.

"My watch gives us twenty minutes more," said Dr. Shallot. "We'd better start moving back toward the ship."

Overstaying their time limit would prove tragic, for a man cannot live more than a minute or so after the supply of oxygen is exhausted. The men started back immediately.

"Let's come out again this afternoon," Jack suggested as they were moving toward the ship. "I'd like to do some more exploring."

"We certainly shall," said the doctor. "There's a lot to find out."

Once inside the ship they removed their pressure suits and replenished the auxiliary compressed air tanks.

As they were checking the equipment after lunch Mr. Warick teased Dr. Shallot.

"That's a beautiful mustache you have there, Doctor. You should be mighty proud of it."

The doctor preened his mustache and strutted a bit. "I'm certainly proud of it. In a few more days I'm going to let you photograph it. I think there should be a picture for historical records, because there will never be another mustache like this one."

After a brief rest the men gathered together their apparatus, put on the pressure suits, and went out of the ship. They hooked themselves together as before. Mr. Warick, in the lead, was carrying a small pick, the kind that geologists use. Jack was carrying a rifle, and Dr. Shallot had the leather specimen pouch hooked to his belt.

They moved directly to the left side of the lens bank and skirted along it in the same way that they had covered the right segment in the morning. As they neared the end, they were puzzled and disappointed, for not a sign of an entrance had they located.

"I can't figure it out," said Mr. Warick. "I was certain we would find a break of some sort."

"I was, too," said Jack without any spirit.

As Jack spoke he looked out beyond the installation and saw a place where the reddish regularity of the terrain was broken by a blackened area.

"Look over there," he cried as he pointed to a place about a hundred yards away. "What do you suppose that black spot is?"

"I don't know," said Dr. Shallot, "but let's find out."

They hurried over to the blackened area. It was not a spot, but a hole at least twelve feet in diameter and thirty feet deep. It was lined with a silver gray metal that appeared to be one unbroken piece. They peered into it but could not see the bottom clearly, although it seemed to be made of the same material as the sides. There was a sturdy metal ladder that extended all the way to the bottom.

"This must be the entrance," exclaimed Mr. Warick. "It looks more and more as though there are people down there."

It was obvious that Dr. Shallot was puzzled as he spoke. "I'm beginning to think you're right. Maybe there are people here, creatures that are very much like us." He was loath to accept the idea, however, and went on, saying, "But how do we know this is an entrance? There still aren't any doors that we can see. Maybe it's a pit of some sort, or a burial place."

"It must be an entrance," said Jack. "Or why would there be a ladder? And who but men could have made it?"

"That's sensible enough," agreed Dr. Shallot.

"Well, let's find out," said Mr. Warick as he moved toward the ladder, "what are we waiting for?"

"Hold on, Don," ordered the leader. "Not so fast. Only one of us should go down. Then the others can follow later. But we'll have to hurry because our oxygen supplies are dwindling rapidly."

It was decided that Mr. Warick should make the first descent. The rope was secured about him, and the doctor and Jack kept a firm hold on the other end. Mr. Warick gripped the top rungs, and clambered over the edge of the pit. Slowly and carefully he went down and down and down. Jack and Dr. Shallot kept their eyes on him every step of the way.

"Do you see anything?"

"Not a thing, just a blank wall."

"Be sure each rung is solid before you put your weight on it. Some of the metal might be corroded."

"Doesn't seem to be," said Mr. Warick as he lowered himself still farther. "Everything is solid."

Then with great excitement he said, "Wait, there's something here. Looks like a door of some sort."

He continued to speak excitedly, "I can't see any hinges, or knobs or any way of opening it. Maybe it's not a door after all. Looks like the entrance to a bank vault."

"Try knocking on it, Don. It may swing free."

"I will, Doctor. Here goes, and won't you be surprised if a Martian invites me in!"

Mr. Warick knocked on the door with the handle of the small pick he was carrying. There was no response.

"Nobody home, I guess. Maybe they're out to the circus."

"Try again," Jack said excitedly. "Maybe if you use

the metal end of the pick it will make a louder sound."

Mr. Warick pounded upon the door heavily but still there was no response.

"I guess there's no one home, or else they don't like visitors," said Mr. Warick with a laugh.

"Look over the door carefully, Don, and maybe you'll find a secret opening device. It could be a vault where the tools of the Martian civilization are stored, like the time capsules we have on earth."

Mr. Warick checked the door inch by inch. As he moved toward the top of it, he exclaimed loudly, "Wow! No need to knock. They know I'm here all right. There are dozens of them, hundreds of them."

"Hundreds of what? What do you see down there?"

"Hundreds of eyes. Hundreds of them staring at me through a misted window that blends into the metal."

"Eyes? Just eyes? Do you mean there's nothing else? No head, or ears? Don, there have to be."

Softly, as though he were speaking to himself, Dr. Shallot said, "How could there be eyes without heads? It's impossible."

Mr. Warick heard all this over his loudspeaker, and he answered forcefully, "No, I tell you it's true. There are no heads. The entire window is covered with eyes, and every last one is staring straight at me, following every movement that I make."

Dr. Shallot would have no more of this. "Come up," he ordered, "come up quickly."

As he spoke, the door slid vertically and hundreds of grotesque figures swarmed over Mr. Warick. Jack and the doctor yanked on the rope, but it came free sickeningly. One of the creatures scrambled up it a few feet and then dropped down.

Before Dr. Shallot and Jack could react, the bottom was cleared. Don Warick was gone and the door was slid back into position.

There were so many of the creatures that Jack could not get a clear picture of them. They seemed to be about four or five feet tall and had unbelievably slender bodies. Their heads were extremely large, so large that it seemed impossible their fragile bodies could hold them up. Jack's strongest memory of them was a sea of huge heads with tiny legs and arms attached. The strangest thing about them was not their heads, but their antennalike eyes. To Jack the eyes appeared to be long, wiry projections on each side of the head. These were the eyes Mr. Warick had seen through the window.

Everything happened so fast that Dr. Shallot and Jack were stunned. One moment they were wondering if there was life on this cold, strange planet; and the next moment they saw that there was life and that it existed abundantly and in great distortion. And one moment Mr.

Warick was conversing gayly with them; the next he was gone, snatched away.

As soon as the door was closed, Jack rushed toward the ladder, intent upon going down to rescue his friend. Dr. Shallot held him back with a firm, friendly hand. "No, Jack," he said strongly, "that won't help. We must hurry back to the ship. Our air supply is short."

There was nothing to do but leave the pit and hurry back to the *Lodestar* for the auxiliary air supply was slipping away rapidly.

Jack's eyes were heavy with tears, for he had grown very close to Mr. Warick. He was not only a crew mate, but he was a dear friend. There was no hope for him, because even if the Martians spared him, he could not live. He must have air, and his supply was almost exhausted when he was taken.

Sadness and disaster had overtaken the *Lodestar*. Dr. Shallot glumly wrote the tragic happenings in the logbook.

The scientist and Jack were drawn closer, for now they were completely dependent upon each other. It was inconceivable that the rocket could be launched by a single person, so the return to earth was possible only if both survived. If the worst happened and either of them died, the other one could live for a long while within the ship; but eventually the food would give out and starvation and death would follow. The situation was desperate indeed. They were two against the universe. As they lay down to sleep that night, they talked of Mr. Warick.

The night was one of turmoil. Jack tossed and turned, trying desperately to sleep but he could not. Occasionally he heard a rustle from the place where Dr. Shallot was lying. He, too, found that sleep was elusive. Neither of them slept more than two hours during the entire night.

In the early hours of morning Jack could stand the tossing no longer, and he called out softly, "Doctor, are you awake?"

The response was immediate, "Yes, Jack. I can't sleep at all."

"Neither can I. Golly, I've been thinking. We can't leave Mr. Warick out there. We just have to go back to that pit to see what happened to him. I could never live with myself if we didn't do something to find out what happened."

"No, neither could I."

"Let's go to the bottom of the pit and get a look at that door. Maybe we'll see the window and be able to look through it."

"It's worth a try, my boy."

"We'll have to work fast, though, unless we can figure out a way of getting more oxygen."

"I think we can solve that all right. We can strap an

extra can on our backs and run a tube into the auxiliary tank. In that way we can get an extra twenty-eight minutes."

As he thought about Mr. Warick, Jack could not help adding, "What a horrible way to die. He must have strangled to death when his air supply gave out."

"Let's not think about that, Jack. There's plenty of work for us to do before we set out. We might better get at it and stop the morbid thinking."

Jack wanted action. He wanted to be doing something, and was glad to get out of bed and work. He wanted mostly to avenge Mr. Warick, and had an overwhelming desire to destroy every one of those weird creatures that had snatched away his friend.

The ship was set to rights, and then they put on their pressure suits. Each of them strapped an extra oxygen tank to his back, picked up a rifle, and went through the escape hatch. They roped themselves together and set a straight course for the pit. Now that they were in action and doing something about their great loss, they both felt better.

The pit looked exactly as it had the day before. From the ground level there was no sign of the struggle that had taken place. Jack and the doctor peered into it for a long time, wondering if the descent should be made. For once they were at the pit, they were not sure that this was the wisest thing to do. But wise or not, both knew that if they did not go down, their minds would never again be at peace.

"Maybe we'll find some other way of getting into the place, Jack, instead of through that door."

"I sure hope so. How I'd like to get my hands on those birds."

At that moment Jack had more courage than discretion. He preceded Dr. Shallot down the ladder. Down, down, down they went. The ladder was solid and firm. They moved along slowly, studying every square inch of the surface; nothing could be seen, however, but solid metal, smoothed and polished.

"I don't see a thing yet, Doctor. Just solid metal."

"That's all I see, Jack. Let's keep going. There may be some sort of entrance that Mr. Warick missed. One that we may be able to force or shoot open."

Jack was skeptical. He had no such hopes as the doctor had.

They reached the bottom of the pit. Directly underneath the ladder was the fateful door. It was a remarkable piece of workmanship for it fitted into the wall so perfectly that only a slight inset was visible.

"Careful now, Jack. Keep your rifle cocked."

"I have it ready, Doctor. Where's that window Mr. Warick saw? The whole door looks like solid metal."

"Yes, I can't see anything that even resembles a window."

"He must have seen a window here somewhere."

"There's no doubt about it, Jack. It's uncanny. Let's go over the door carefully, inch by inch."

They moved very close to the door, close enough to touch it.

"Look out," yelled Jack. "Doctor, look out, eyes, the eyes, hundreds of them."

They leaped back from the door.

"Hundreds of them? It looks more as though there were thousands. And they're staring straight at us."

The sight was weird and unbelievable.

"I'm going to fire at them," Jack said as he raised his rifle and leveled it at the window which seemed to be alive with eyes.

The doctor pushed the rifle out of position and said, "That won't help at all, Jack. We'll have to figure out a way of dealing with those fellows."

Jack lowered the rifle. As he did so, the door flashed upward and the Martians swarmed over them. Jack tried to bring his rifle into play, but it was no use. There were hundreds of the creatures. They covered the ladder, the floor of the pit, and the walls. Jack could not move an arm, leg, or a single muscle. He called to his companion. Over and over again he called, "Dr. Shallot, Dr. Shallot, can you hear me?" He was screaming the name, but there was no response. It was hideous, he thought, having these weird creatures swarm all over him, and being unable to fight them off. He began to feel faint. His eyes were hazing and he could see nothing but red. He was drifting away. The last thing he remembered was hearing his name called faintly, far off in the distance. Had he been able to think, he probably would have assumed it was the angel Gabriel calling him to the Promised Land.

"Jack, Jack, Jack," he heard. Over and over again the name echoed through his head. The tone was soft, almost tender. It reminded him of home. He thought of his mother, and pictured her at work in their kitchen baking an apple pie with cinnamon, his favorite of them all.

Jack heard the voice again, this time calling more firmly. "Jack," it said, "wake up, wake up."

With great effort, not quite knowing what he was doing, Jack opened his eyes slightly, and there before him, bending over him, was Don Warick.

Mr. Warick?

"No, no," he thought, "it can't be Mr. Warick. I'm still dreaming."

Jack closed his eyes quickly. Soon he heard the voice again.

"You're all right, Jack. Open your eyes. It's Don, Don Warick. Open your eyes."

Jack struggled for consciousness, forcing his eyes open. And there he was again. It was Mr. Warick, there was no doubt about it. Jack reached out a hand to touch him.

"Mr. Warick?" he questioned weakly and with disbelief.

"Yes, Jack, it's me. Who'd you think it was?"

"I, I don't know. We thought you were dead. When they got you we thought it was all over."

"The pixies got me all right, Jack. But I'm not dead, believe me. They can't get rid of us that easy."

"What happened? Where are we? Where's Dr. Shallot?" asked Jack. As he was asking the questions Jack noticed that Mr. Warick was wearing no globe. He felt his own head and neck. He was wearing none either.

"Where are our globes? How can we breathe without them?"

"We don't need them, Jack. These little people keep oxygen moving around down here all the time. But you can't exert yourself much, or you'll tire out in no time. There's enough oxygen for them, but not nearly enough for us."

"That means that these Martians are animals pretty much like those on earth," said Jack. And then he remembered their leader. "Where's Dr. Shallot?" he asked. "What happened to him?"

"He's right behind you. He was banged up pretty badly. Must have put up quite a battle." They moved to the doctor, who was lying on the floor, and rubbed his wrists and temples. The older man moaned softly but would not open his eyes or speak, in spite of all their efforts. His pulse and breathing were even and regular, so there was nothing they could do for him until he regained consciousness.

Jack's head was full of questions, and his heart was full of joy at finding Mr. Warick alive and well.

"Maybe you'd better not be too happy about it, Jack," he said in a puzzling manner.

"Why not?"

"Because I can't figure out these birds. They've had me in this room ever since they dragged me out of the pit. They just brought me in, set me down gently, and walked away. There were so many of them it would have been foolish to fight them."

"You're telling me," said Jack. "There must be hundreds of them, and they get all over you so fast you don't have a chance. Before you know what's happening, it's all over."

"Every now and then two or three of them come in here. They jibber-jabber back and forth, poke at me sometimes, jump and leap about, and out they go again. I can't figure out what they're up to."

"What are they like close up?" asked Jack as he continued to massage the doctor's wrists. And then he added, "I sure wish he'd come to."

"Wait," said Mr. Warick. "Look."

As he spoke, the soft lights of the barren room became brighter. Jack could now see that the walls were of solid rock that was as smoothed and polished as were the walls of the outside pit. The ceiling was made of the same material; it was a rock that resembled granite or basalt.

"What does the bright light mean?"

"It means they're coming, I think. That's what it meant before."

Jack was greatly excited at the idea of seeing these creatures close to him when he didn't have to fight them. His curiosity was much stronger than his dread.

"Don't do anything at all when they come in, Jack. They're not very pleasant to look at, but they won't harm us if we don't go after them."

An identical pair of round heads entered the room. They did have bodies; but it was the round heads that impressed Jack more than anything else. There was no hair on their heads. They were as smooth as an egg, and just about as white. There were small ears on either side of the head, two piglike eyes, a flat nose, and a tiny round mouth. Both of the faces were expressionless. Later the men came to realize that all the Martians are emotionless—at least they had no emotions that could be noticed —so their faces were complete blanks. They did not smile or frown; their eyes did not sparkle nor their noses dilate. Thus it was difficult to tell one from the other. Only in their mannerisms did they differ. But this method was far from foolproof as they were to find on numerous occasions.

Protruding from the top of the grotesque heads were antennae, one from each side, and in line with the pig-like eyes. One antenna was tipped with an eye that rolled about, and the other ended in what looked like a brass ball about a half inch in diameter.

The creatures did not move. They stood still and stared straight at the men from the *Lodestar*. Although the small eyes looked ahead, the large antenna eye twisted and turned, looking forward and backward and all around. Jack could not tell where the creatures were looking, or what kind of an impression he was making on them.

The bodies were remarkably well proportioned, although they were much too small for the heads. The Martians wore no clothing at all, but were covered by a soft growth, somewhat between hair and fur in texture. Their fingers were fine and delicate. There were no toes on the small, padded feet.

As Mr. Warick had said they would, the heads bobbed back and forth and jumped around. One of the Martians came toward Jack. Jack moved away but he kept coming toward him.

"It's all right, Jack," said Mr. Warick. "They only want to touch you."

Jack stopped moving and allowed the creature to come near enough to touch him. Once this was done, the Martian seemed satisfied and jibbered in a soft murmur to its companion. As he moved away Jack could smell a pleasant odor, a clean, sweet smell.

The creatures seemed to have satisfied their curiosity for they moved back along the corridor. When they were out of sight, the lights dimmed again.

While the Martians were in the room Jack's interest had left Dr. Shallot, but now he rested his hand on the doctor's pulse. It was considerably stronger.

Jack exhaled deeply. "Wow," he said, "did you ever see anything so ugly in your life?"

"They certainly aren't pretty, are they?"

"It's weird the way that eye wiggles around on the end of the antenna. It gives me the creeps. What's the other thing for—the brassy looking ball?"

"You've got me, Jack. It looks like a radio aerial of some sort, but it's impossible that an aerial could be part of the body."

Impossible, yes, by earth standards. But later on the men learned that the brass ball was just that. It was a radio antenna. In the same way that earth bodies produce sound and heat, the bodies of the Martians were able to produce radio frequencies. And in the same way that earth bodies can receive light, sound, and heat, their bodies could receive and interpret radio signals. Each individual could send out weak radio beams similar to a brain wave that would carry several hundred yards. Signals like these were used to open doors, regulate light intensity, control the temperature in the underground rooms, and operate numerous appliances. And each individual could pick up signals through his natural antenna. Thus the entire population could be alerted or directed to act in a second. That was why so many of them swarmed on the men so quickly when they were captured.

Then the lights brightened as they did before.

"Not again, I hope," said Jack as he looked at the luminous ceiling, and peered down the passage.

"It looks like more visitors," said Mr. Warick.

There was a shuffling along the corridor. Four Martians moved into the room, carrying two large metal slabs. From the manner in which they walked, it was apparent that the slabs were heavy. They set them on the floor, turned around and left without looking to the right or left. Only their antenna eyes twisted about.

"What's this?" Jack asked as he looked toward the slabs.

"That, my good friend," said Mr. Warick with a flourish, "is food."

"Food?" said Jack. "I'd have welcomed them if I'd known that. Let's hope it's tasty."

"You're in for a surprise, Jack." Mr. Warick looked closely at Dr. Shallot. "His eyes are opening," he said. "I guess he's going to be all right."

They continued to massage their leader's neck, wrists, and temples, and he gradually showed more signs of consciousness. Jack, rather than Mr. Warick, talked to him because they feared the shock would be too great if he saw Mr. Warick while he was still dazed. After a few minutes he recovered enough to speak. Slowly the story was unfolded to him, and the happy threesome were united. The experiences they had been through were trying and dangerous; but now that they were three again the horror of those moments was forgotten.

The situation was still dark. Fortunately all the controls of the *Lodestar* were properly set. The ship would maintain its temperature during the cold Martian night and would not freeze. The ship caused them no worry on that score; but they were anxious about their capture and the immediate future.

Mr. Warick, with his good humor and judgment, which always came to the fore when they were in trouble, suggested that since there was food they might as well eat it.

"After we have fed ourselves and are more comfortable, we can worry some more," he said. "Right now I'm too hungry to worry."

They gathered around the large trays, and Mr. Warick raised the metal covers with great ceremony. He uncovered a beautiful display of wonderful foods. There was nothing on the trays exactly like food on earth, but many of the items were similar. There were succulent grapelike fruits that grew in clusters, and juicy red objects about the size and texture of tomatoes. The interior of these was not full of seeds, as are tomatoes, but was solid and chewy. Here and there were berrylike objects that were very juicy and strong in flavor. The red tomatolike fruit was apparently the staple food, since it was the most abundant. It had been two months since they had seen fresh food, so they ate with gusto and cleared the trays.

They had no way of knowing what the Martians had in store for them; but obviously the strange creatures did not plan to starve them.

10. THE SENTENCE

IT WAS IMPERATIVE that some way of escape be found. Even if their lives were to be spared, they could not go on living in the Martian underground. This would mean failure of their mission.

"But escape is out of the question," said Mr. Warick. "In the first place we can't get out of here. There is no way to get out of this room except through that narrow passageway. And I believe it's guarded as closely as our launching site was. If we moved along it, we'd be spotted immediately. And even if we were able to open those trick doors and get outside, we'd die without our pressure suits. Escape won't work. We'll have to find a better way."

"Well, then," said Dr. Shallot, rubbing his temple, "we'll have to gain their confidence so they'll return the suits and let us out of here."

"But how can you gain the confidence of such creatures? We can't make head or tail of their language. They don't even move their mouths or lips when they talk. They only make those eerie singsong sounds deep in their throats."

"It will take time, Don, there's no doubt of that. It's a slim chance that we ever will get them to believe in us; but it's our only chance to get out of here, so we must try."

"We haven't the slightest idea what they plan to do with us," said Jack. "For that matter, maybe they're friendly now, and will let us go whenever we want to. Or maybe they think we're gods of some sort."

"Maybe so, Jack, let's hope you're right."

As the doctor spoke, a shuffling was heard in the corridor. Jack hurried toward it. At first he could see nothing, but as they came closer he could see a seemingly endless file of Martians parading toward their room.

The men watched the Martians take the little steps that brought them closer and closer. As before, the faces were like those of statues, pasty white and expressionless, so the men had no way of knowing whether their captors were pleased or angry.

But for the crew the processional was grim, and it troubled them. They became tense as the column approached. They were expecting the worst to happen.

As the file came closer, the doctor said quietly but firmly, keeping his eyes on the Martians, "Do whatever they wish, and do it willingly. We must convince them that we are friendly."

About twenty of the creatures surrounded the crew, and by pushing and pointing and prodding, let them know that they wanted the men to move along the hallway. One of them led the way.

Because Mr. Warick had been underground longer, Jack asked him, "Where do you suppose we're going?"

"Haven't the slightest idea," Mr. Warick answered. "We could be going to a reception of welcome." He sunk his hands into his pockets, shrugged his shoulders, and added, "Or we could be going to our execution."

As they walked along, Jack noticed the lighting. There were no electric bulbs of any sort, yet light was everywhere. Not much in some places, but always enough to give a soft glow to the surroundings. Apparently fluorescent materials in the rock were made to glow by radiant energy supplied to them, in much the same way that fluorescent tubes glow when radiant waves strike them.

Dr. Shallot, Mr. Warick, and Jack walked abreast of each other behind the Martian who was leading. Behind them were twenty or more Martians in a loose, double column. The column looked like a guard of execution, not like a friendly procession. Jack's jaws were clenched and his fingers tense.

"Looks pretty bad," Jack whispered to Mr. Warick.

"Sure does," he answered quietly, "just have to hope for the best."

"Quiet, you two," ordered their leader.

Here and there along the corridor they saw vaultlike doors like the one in the pit. After walking about an eighth of a mile, the procession stopped in front of one of these doors. The Martian leader stepped forward. As he did so, the door slid up quickly and silently.

Before them the men saw a vast, cathedral-like auditorium. They forgot for a minute that they were underground, so spacious was the hall. The walls and ceiling glowed intensely with a smooth irridescent light. The ceiling was a graceful arch which started about nine feet above the floor. Jack looked quickly at the highest point and decided that it was about seventy-five feet high. He realized that the passage through which they had walked must have slanted, although the decline was so gradual that it was not apparent. In spite of the great height and length of the hall, there were no supporting posts. Wonderful engineers, Jack said to himself. There was no decoration in the entire place other than that produced by the lighting. The men noticed also that there was no cold or damp feeling. The temperature was comfortable. A warm glow seemed to radiate through the hall. It was a majestic auditorium, worthy of the efforts of earth's greatest architects. The men from the *Lodestar* were overwhelmed by the sight before them, and they stood frozen in their tracks.

Seated on the floor, with their backs to the entrance, were thousands of Martians. Jack could smell the same odor that he had noticed before. It hung over the hall like a fog.

The Martian leader walked ahead slowly. Pressure from behind pushed the men after him. Jack and Mr. Warick looked toward Dr. Shallot. He nodded his head, and they accepted his decision to continue on their way. They realized that to resist was suicide.

The auditorium was as wide as a city block, and as long as two football fields placed end to end. Slowly, and in complete silence, the men marched along the aisle that divided the Martians into two groups. The head of each Martian was held erect so their eyes were straight ahead. But the antenna eyes were twisting about on their wiry extensions and following every movement the men made.

"Gives you the willies," Jack said quietly.

"It certainly does," whispered Mr. Warick. "I don't like the way those eyes twist around. Makes you feel as though they were looking right through you."

"Better keep quiet," cautioned the doctor softly, "they may not like the talking."

They thought they were being led into a trap. Jack expected the throng to swarm over them at any minute, as when they had been captured. Every muscle of his body was tensed, ready for the attack. His teeth and jaws were pressed together tightly as they strode straight ahead without turning their heads to either the right or left. The air was heavy with the clean, sweet smell of the Martians. At other times the odor had been pleasant, but now it sickened him because it was so heavy.

Walking so far in the thin air of the underground was very tiring, but they forced themselves to keep going. Finally the center of the hall was reached. They mounted a stagelike platform where three Martians, apparently the leaders, were standing. The crew were pushed toward the center of the circular platform. The group that had brought them from their prison room stood on the main floor with their backs toward the platform.

Suddenly the thousands gathered there broke into weird singing. The sound was between a whine and a moan, and it made Jack's flesh crawl. The music lasted for a minute or so and then stopped suddenly.

One of the three Martians on the platform glided to the front and bowed deeply.

As he did, a kind of cheer went up from the multitude. To Jack it sounded like "Mugs" or "Maugs." It began very loudly and quieted down gradually until there was complete silence—dead silence, so still that Jack could hear his own breathing.

"That must be the big man," Jack whispered to Mr. Warick. "What now?"

"Who knows?" he answered out of the side of his mouth.

There was no chance to speak further, for one of the group that had brought the men to the hall stepped to the platform. He spoke rapidly in a quiet, squeaky monotone to the one called Mugs. As he talked he gestured toward the crew with his thin arms. From time to time a whine went up from the audience. Then he returned to his place.

Jack looked at Dr. Shallot. The older man's face was rigid, and his cheeks were very drawn in. Mr. Warick, however, in spite of the tense situation, had relaxed somewhat, and was watching the proceedings with intense interest. Jack was far from relaxed. He still expected an attack.

Several more members of the escort group stepped to the platform, one at a time, pointed long, graceful fingers at the men and delivered squeaky tirades. Every time one spoke, the Martians joined in the singing whine, though it was not as loud as the first time.

"What do you make of it, Doctor?"

Dr. Shallot's disbelief in the spectacle before him was so great that he spoke with great difficulty. "I—I—it looks like a trial, Jack. Here comes the boss again."

Mugs spoke in the same shrill voice the others had used. When he had finished, there was bedlam.

This is it, thought Jack. And he said aloud, "They're working up to something."

"Just hold tight, Jack. Don't make a move, and maybe we'll get out of here with a whole skin," whispered Dr. Shallot.

Their escorts came to the platform and prodded the men forward. They walked through a silent mass of heads the long way back to the door through which they had entered. Not a creature touched them, but every one of them stared with his small round eyes as they passed, and they all scrambled to get close to the crew. The antennae were waving about grotesquely like a multitude of serpents standing on their tails. To Jack it was a nightmare.

Soon the men were in the corridor and were being led back in the direction from which they had come.

"Whew," said Jack, exhaling deeply, "I never thought we'd get out of there alive."

"Neither did I," said Dr. Shallot. "Things looked pretty bad at times."

"They're a queer lot," said Mr. Warick. They took a few steps in silence, then he added, "But you know, I'm beginning to like those fellows. I'll bet that if we could talk their langauge we'd find they're not so bad after all."

When they got back to their room, the men discussed every phase of what they had gone through. None of them was able to explain the proceedings, although they were quite sure it was a trial of some sort. Whether there had been a verdict they did not know; and they still did not know whether they were prisoners of the Martians or were honored guests.

Days went by. The crew discussed their trial over and over again, taking each event and pulling it apart in search of a clue that would give them some idea of what was to happen. They talked about the passage through which they had walked, and the fabulous hall where the trial was held.

"Why," said Mr. Warick as he furrowed his brow, "do you realize how much rock had to be removed to make that hall?"

They all realized that the auditorium was a thing of wonder, that hundreds of thousands of tons of rock had been moved to make it. But their amazement over the size of the task was not as great as their consternation when later on they learned how the work was done. The Martians had developed every aspect of radio, and had used it to solve many of their problems—even those involving manual labor.

A long while after their capture, the men found that a

plan was drawn of the solid rock as it appeared before any work was started. Then a plan was made of the auditorium as it would look when roughed out; finally a third plan showed the finished hall.

These plans were placed in an electronic device where they were scanned by a battery of electric eyes. The electric eyes relayed impulses to a radio mechanism that controlled drilling rigs, dump cars, sand blasters, and polishing wheels. An area that was to be removed was shaded on the drawing. When the electric eye hit the shading it activated those drills and cars located in the area comparable to the shaded area of the drawing. In this and similar ways radio did most of the work of the Martians. In fact, the whole auditorium was made by only six Martians. And their work was not difficult, since it consisted merely of adjusting the radio controls and supervising the work of the robot mechanisms.

Sleeping for the men was very difficult. There were no mattresses and they had to lie on solid rock. What sleep they could get was fitful and crowded with nightmares. One night Jack had a terrible dream. He felt that he was in a burning building from which there was no escape. The room filled with smoke, and he had great difficulty in breathing. He was gagging and choking; tears were running from his eyes. He awoke to find it was no dream, for he was wheezing and his lungs felt as though they were about to burst. Dr. Shallot and Mr. Warick, both of whom were gagging also, dragged Jack to his feet.

"Stand up," they said as they placed him upright. "Try to stand, and you'll get more air."

"I thought I was gagging from smoke," Jack said as he rubbed his eyes and breathed deeply.

"You were gagging but not from smoke. You weren't getting enough oxygen," Mr. Warick explained.

They were sleeping far to the right of the entrance to the corridor. Since oxygen was not circulated as well at night as in the daytime, the corner was a pocket that did not get as much fresh atmosphere as did other parts of the room. Dr. Shallot moved slowly around the hall and then decided that a place directly in front of the passageway would contain the richest oxygen supply. He was right, and after that experience there were no more incidents of near suffocation.

When Jack awoke on the fifth morning after their capture, he saw that Mr. Warick and Dr. Shallot were still asleep. He raised himself to a sitting position, rubbed his arms and legs, and looked about. A Martian was leaning over their leader and his great head almost touched Dr. Shallot's. Jack's first impulse was to jump up and knock him away. But he held himself back, for there was something about the stance of the creature that made him look harmless. Jack looked more closely. The Martian was not touching the doctor but only looking at him intently. Jack watched him several minutes in complete silence, trying to decide what the Martian was doing. And then he knew. It was the mustache! The Martians had no whiskers at all, and their visitor was entranced by Dr. Shallot's. He stood in a bent, uncomfortable posture and stared at it.

Dr. Shallot was making small motions, and showing other signs of wakefulness. Jack feared that if he were to open his eyes and see that grotesque face within inches of his own, he would be startled and might strike the Martian. So before the doctor awoke, Jack called to him softly. The sound of his voice didn't affect the Martian at all, for he showed no sign that he had heard it. Jack told his leader that a Martian was hanging over him and that he should not be alarmed. Dr. Shallot opened his eyes slowly, and when he did the Martian touched them. Dr. Shallot winced, but kept calm. Then the Martian touched the mustache gingerly. A touch was all that he wanted apparently, for he then straightened up ponderously and moved down the corridor rapidly and silently.

"I wonder how long he's been around?" asked Dr. Shallot as he got to his feet and smoothed his clothing.

"A long time, I think," Jack said as he pushed back his hair, "I've been watching him for several minutes."

When Mr. Warick awoke they told him what had happened. He roared with laughter as he spoke. "You see, Doctor, I told you that mustache was irresistible. Now maybe you'll believe me. When they hang over you to admire it, you can be mighty proud of yourself. That mustache will go down in history with Lincoln's beard and Grant's whiskers."

"Perhaps so," said Dr. Shallot smilingly, "but when I awoke and saw that Martian leaning over me, I wished I had never grown the thing. It's well you told me about him, Jack, or I think I might have jumped up and knocked him off his feet. And that wouldn't have made it any easier for us to make friends."

The mustache became the key to friendship as curiosity got the better of the Martian. Time and time again he returned to admire the mustache, and through it, he and Dr. Shallot became friendly. The men knew that this fellow could do much for them, but their problem was to find some way to communicate with him. After many attempts they gave up trying to learn his language, for they could make no sense of it. It seemed wiser to build a new way to exchange ideas.

Dr. Shallot took it upon himself to do this. He started by making simple one-syllable sounds, no more than musical tones. When he made what sounded like middle *a*, he pointed to himself. The Martian registered no reaction but amusement. This went on for hours, and even days, yet no progress was made. Or so it seemed. But one day the Martian entered the room, made the sound of *a* and walked directly toward Dr. Shallot. They were overjoyed.

From this humble beginning Dr. Shallot developed a language known only to himself and this friendly Martian who was called Mahkee, since this was the first sound which seemed to give him pleasure. Their language at first consisted of various musical tones. Later it came to include one-syllable expressions such as *puh, wush, wok, ling, sut,* and *hak.* The doctor recorded these sounds in his small notebook, and they will probably become the basis for an interplanetary tongue, should such a language become necessary.

Many arduous days passed before Dr. Shallot was able to learn anything from Mahkee. And when their friend was able to communicate what the Martians had decided to do, the report did not make pleasant listening. The men were to be kept in prison forever, never to be released from the barren, rock-bound room. This was their prison. Such was the sentence that the great one, the one called Mugs, had imposed. And since it had been agreed to by the great assembly of all the Martian population, there could be no change. This was the penalty.

"Penalty? For what?" asked Jack scornfully. "What did we do?"

"It isn't what we did that bothers them," said Dr. Shallot, "it's what we planned to do. Mahkee says that Mugs, the great one, told the Martians that we came to destroy them, to shadow the life-giving lenses and cast everlasting darkness over them. And he told them that it was only good luck that we were captured, and the population was still alive."

"Well, now," said Mr. Warick, "that's a pretty kettle of fish. Mugs certainly has it in for us." And then he added, "What about Mahkee. Can't he do anything for us?"

"I don't know yet," answered Dr. Shallot. "We'll have to move cautiously. If we push him too much, we'll ruin everything we've gained. All our hopes rest upon him, so we'll have to make progress slowly."

They could not understand why they were fed so well, or why the Martians didn't kill them if they were believed to be so dangerous; but Dr. Shallot dared not ask Mahkee. Later they learned that the Martians would not kill for any reason whatsoever. They respected life highly, and every death in the community was a personal tragedy. To deprive any creature of adequate food would be against their high moral standards. These were two Martian viewpoints with which the men agreed heartily!

The story that Mahkee told made their future look very black. They knew that only by having Dr. Shallot convince the Martians of the true reasons that they were on the planet could they be freed. After many stumbling and fruitless efforts, he succeeded in explaining their mission to Mahkee—or so he believed. But days went by and there was no change in their status. They continued to be held in their rocky jail room, and they found it increasingly easy to surrender hope and give in to despair.

They were given plenty of food, although the water was doled out in small, measured amounts. But their quota was sufficient to maintain health, since many of the foods contained a high percentage of water, which made up the difference.

They were aggravated most, however, by their inability to determine time. When they went to sleep they did not know whether it was night or day. All of their lives they carried on certain activities when the sun reached various positions. They had risen when the sun was in the east, had lunched when it was overhead, had gone home when the sun was in the west and had slept when it was below the horizon. Now life was different. They had nothing to use that would help them orient themselves, for there was nothing they could see but the blank walls of their room. Dr. Shallot had kept his watch running, fortunately, so they knew when an hour had passed, and even longer periods of time; but they could not determine whether it was day or night, nor did they know when a new day had begun. But even with these failings, the watch was an aid in keeping up their morale, for it gave them a hold on time, weak as that hold was.

They spent many long hours in computing the number of days that had passed since their capture. Their estimates ran from ten days to sixteen days, depending upon whether they were in good spirits or bad when the figuring was being done.

"If something doesn't happen soon," said Mr. Warick one day as they were trying to remember how many meals had been eaten, "I'm going to make a break for it. A few more days cooped up in here will drive me crazy."

They still used the word "day," although the word had no real significance for them.

"Take it easy, Don," said Dr. Shallot calmly. "At least we're still alive. And as long as we are, and are feeling well, we can hope for something better."

"I don't see how we're going to stay healthy in this place," replied Mr. Warick. "I'm thinking it would be better to have it out with the little fellows."

"We're all getting edgy," said Dr. Shallot. He knew this was a crucial time, for the success of the mission and the hope for release lay in solidarity. He rubbed his temple vigorously and then smiled.

"Why don't we rig up a chess set?" he asked. "Maybe we can take the champion honors away from Don."

"Good," exclaimed Jack happily, "a chess game would

be perfect." But this happiness didn't last very long. "How can we? We haven't anything to start with."

"Sure we have," said Mr. Warick who was so pleased with the idea that he was grinning widely. "We can use buttons and matches and anything else you happen to have on you."

They rifled their pockets and tore buttons from their clothing to get objects that could be used for chessmen. They gathered sixteen assorted buttons, washers, pieces of wire, and cotter pins that were used for pawns. Dr. Shallot tore pieces of paper from the memo pad he always carried. The rooks, bishops, horses, kings, and queens were represented by initial letters on these scraps; an *R* for a rook, *K* for the king, and so on.

Once they had all the pieces, the only thing they lacked was a board. Dr. Shallot solved this problem, too. He took off his jacket and laid it on the floor. He then laid out the sixty-four squares of a chess board, shading in half of them with his pencil.

Playing on a cloth board with pieces that were much alike was not easy. But the obstacles served to make the men concentrate harder, and their minds were on the game completely. A tournament was established and scores were kept accurately. Chess proved to bring them more happiness than anything short of their return to the *Lodestar*.

11. A MARTIAN FARM

AFTER WHAT SEEMED to be many weeks, Mahkee brought good news. Although the sentence had not been changed, and they would continue to be held captive, the crew would be allowed to visit other parts of the Martian underground. This news was almost as good as a reprieve, for they were starving for a change of scenery and for activity. When Dr. Shallot interpreted Mahkee's message, Jack and Mr. Warick were overjoyed. The boy's first impulse was to jump up and go, but he held off long enough to gather together the "chessmen" and place them in a pocket of the doctor's jacket. They left immediately with Mahkee leading the way.

They were like children going to the circus, so great was the relief from boredom. Now they would have another chance to get their bearings, which would be a step, however small, toward the *Lodestar*. And they would learn some more about life on Mars.

They first visited a farm. When the doctor announced that this was their goal, they did not know what to expect. They had had plenty of good food to eat, though it was strange to their palates, but none of them had any idea where their food came from. The only farms Jack knew were the commercial farms of America and the kitchen gardens of suburbanites. He couldn't picture either of these on Mars. And neither of them did he find.

Mahkee led them along the now familiar corridor. When they had moved about a hundred yards, and had passed one door on the left and two on the right, they stopped before the next one.

Dr. Shallot, Mr. Warick, and Jack stood abreast of each other, and Mahkee was slightly in front of them. They could see the back of his bald, white head, and the brown, shiny hair that covered his entire body. As they stood there, the door rose quickly and silently, with no apparent signal from Mahkee.

They were dazzled by a brilliant light, almost as if they were looking at the sun; and they smelled a clean, fresh odor like that given off by newly plowed fields. As they stepped through the door, their eyes were drawn toward the ceiling by the brightness. It was blinding.

"Wow," Jack exclaimed as he squinted his eyes, "I can't see a thing."

"Neither can I," said Mr. Warick, as he shaded his eyes

with his hands and twisted his face. "It's the brightest thing we've seen since we were captured."

"I wonder how they make it?"

Dr. Shallot's question went unanswered at the moment; but later they found that one of the lens banks that they had seen on the surface was directly above this farm. The bank itself formed the ceiling. When sunlight fell on the lenses, the glass softened and diffused it, and distributed it evenly throughout the installation.

When they lowered their eyes they saw row upon row of robust, heavy plants, eight to ten feet high, that were laden with thick, glistening deep green leaves, and bushels of the tomatolike fruit they knew so well. The bushes were supported on a lattice work of green metal. The plants threw out tendrils, much as a grapevine does, and these curled about the metal frame. They were most amazed by the fact that there was no soil. The roots were immersed in tanks of liquid which ran along each of the rows. The rows themselves were about three hundred feet long, and from where they were standing, Jack was able to count twenty-two of them.

A crew of Martians was moving slowly up and down the rows in a four-wheeled cart that ran along silently. They were picking the fruit and placing them in large trays with great care. The picker was made of two pipes six inches in diameter that swung along underneath the fruit and sucked each one into it. One Martian operated each one of the picking tubes, and two others were busy setting the picked fruit into position.

They watched the pickers move along an aisle between two rows of bushes. At the farther end were plants in all stages of growth, from tiny seedlings to full size. Mahkee stared at the seedlings, and indicated that they were to watch closely. They kept their eyes glued to a plant. As they watched, they saw a leaf bud break open and unfold. They gasped. How could anything grow so rapidly? They continued to watch, and by the time they were ready to leave, the plant had gained four or five inches in height.

"How can they do it?" Jack asked incredulously of no one in particular. "How can those plants possibly grow so fast?"

No one paid any attention to his question. Each of the men was too absorbed in his surroundings. Later on part of the answer was found when they visited the laboratory.

Mahkee conducted them into a small, compact laboratory just off the farm. Here they saw another Martian, intent on preparing the chemical mixtures for the solution that was fed to the plants. He worked with great skill and precision.

When he had completed the mixture, the chemist placed it in a receptacle which opened into the main pipe to the root troughs. Distilled water was supplied to the roots. As the water passed under the receptacle, a measured amount of the mixture dripped into it. In this way the roots were supplied constantly with a fresh supply of nutrient material.

The water was returned to the laboratory through other conduits which carried it into huge retorts where it was distilled. The impurities it contained were analyzed, sorted, and bagged, since many of them could be utilized again after they had been refined. The Martians wasted nothing. Everything was used, and used, and used again.

While Mr. Warick and Jack were watching this master chemist, Dr. Shallot and Mahkee were conversing rapidly in their melodious tongue. Mahkee was doing most of the talking and Dr. Shallot listened with astonishment.

There were no sounds at the farm except an occasional clink of the chemist's tools, many of which resembled those used on earth. They also heard the slight plopping made by the picking machine whenever it sucked in a fruit. Everything was so still that Jack thought he heard the plants strain and push as they forced themselves upward toward the lighted ceiling. He knew that such sounds were possible for when he was a boy he had gone into a lush corn patch and had heard the leaves of the cornstalks unfurl as the miracle of growth was re-enacted.

Mahkee directed them back toward the door through

which they had entered. They returned to the prison room rejuvenated, and thanked Mahkee for his kindness.

The wonders they had seen freed their tongues, and they all talked at once.

"Did you ever see such strong plants?"

"And the way they grew. At that rate you'd have a fully grown tree a couple of years after you planted it."

"It's remarkable," said Dr. Shallot. "I wouldn't believe it if I hadn't seen it with my own eyes."

"How can they do it?" asked Mr. Warick. "There must be a secret that they hold."

"When Mahkee was talking to me, he was telling me something that I can't believe. I think he said that the Martians have found precisely how a plant grows. It has always been a mystery how a green leaf can take simple things like carbon dioxide and water and put them together to make carbohydrates. I think the Martians have solved that mystery. And if they know how and why a plant grows, they can feed it what it needs, and in the exact amounts for maximum growth."

"That's something we'll have to take back with us," said Mr. Warick. And then with respect, he added, "These Martians are a lot more clever than I thought at first. They're ahead of us in many ways."

"They sure are," agreed Jack. "Did you see the way that chemist worked? And did you see the clever apparatus for distilling the returned water? Why, they were handling as much water in a two-by-four distillery as we could with one ten times as big."

"Yes, they're clever all right," said Mr. Warick. "We know that because our prison here is completely foolproof. There's nothing but solid rock around us, and that narrow corridor to move through. And those doors! No one could force them even if he had tools to work with."

"Escape certainly is out of the question," said Dr. Shallot. "If we didn't believe so before, we now must. I saw no more than you did, nothing but rock and those infernally clever radio-controlled doors."

"Don't you think we can get Mahkee to help us?" asked Jack hopefully.

"I don't think so," said Dr. Shallot. "These Martians have a strong feeling of loyalty, and I'm afraid he would rather see us disappointed than betray his people."

"Maybe we can work it from another angle then," said Mr. Warick. "Maybe we can convince him that he would be doing the community a great service if he aided us in getting away from here. We aren't doing them any good at all. In fact, all we do is eat their food and breathe their oxygen. If they were rid of us, their limited supplies would stretch farther."

"That sounds good," said Jack. "And if they would let

us go back to the *Lodestar,* they could keep us under guard right up until the time we took off."

"Well, maybe—" said Dr. Shallot doubtfully.

"Mahkee will do anything if you let him stroke your mustache," said Mr. Warick, half seriously and half jokingly.

Dr. Shallot smiled. "Perhaps he will, Don. I'll see what I can do with him." He stretched out on the floor. "I'll try to convince him of our good will, but now I'm going to rest a few minutes. That walk tired me out."

"Ah—before you get too comfortable, Dr. Shallot," said Jack, "may we trouble you for your jacket? Mr. Warick and I will go on with the tournament while you're napping."

When Mahkee visited them again, Dr. Shallot told him about the *Lodestar* and about their desire to return to it. He drew pictures of the rocket and talked a long time to explain that they had come from space, from another planet, that they had been traveling for months and they wanted to return. It was difficult for Mahkee to converse with the doctor about the rocket and earth since there were no words in the language they had built for the rocket, space, and for other planets.

Mahkee showed no sign of understanding whatever. And to make matters worse, he rose abruptly and left the room as though he had been insulted.

"Oh, oh," groaned Mr. Warick, "what did you say to him?"

"Nothing," said Dr. Shallot wonderingly, "not a thing that should hurt his feelings and make him leave like that."

"Maybe you said something that's taboo."

"I hardly think so. They don't believe in that sort of humbug."

No matter what had caused the departure, Mahkee seemed to have been insulted, and their hopes were forlorn, indeed.

But just as abruptly as he had gone, Mahkee returned. He laid before the amazed men dozens of full-color photographs of the *Lodestar*. The pictures were printed on a soft matte substance that resembled both paper and plastic. There were photos of the ship as they were circling Mars in the deceleration runs, pictures of the landing, and numerous shots of the men as they were leaving the *Lodestar* and as they were shuffling through the Martian dust.

"So," said Mr. Warick, when he had recovered from his shock, "they knew all along that we were here. I guess we were lucky to get by as long as we did without being captured."

"It just shows how wise they are, Don. They knew that

we would enter the pit sooner or later. And once we were in it, they knew they could snare us easily."

"They must have cameras hidden all over the place," said Mr. Warick.

"I'll bet I know what they do," said Jack, who was going through the photos busily. "Some of those lenses must be hooked to cameras that automatically photograph every image that falls upon it."

"Maybe so," said Dr. Shallot, "but no matter how they do it, these pictures are a surprise." He gathered them together. "I'll see if I can make some progress with Mahkee. These pictures should make it a little easier."

When he heard his name, Mahkee moved closer to Dr. Shallot. The leader pointed to a picture which showed the *Lodestar* as it appeared in the location where it had been left. He then pointed to himself, indicating that the ship was his. He pointed to Mr. Warick, and then to the ship; and to Jack and then to the ship.

They did not know whether Mahkee understood or not. This disarmed the crew, for they never knew what sort of impression they were making.

Mahkee picked up the pictures and left. After he had gone, Dr. Shallot discussed their progress. He thought that the men had made an impression upon Mahkee, one strong enough to persuade him to help them get back to the *Lodestar*. Mr. Warick was not quite so optimistic.

"Suppose we did make an impression upon him," said Mr. Warick. "What can he do to help us? How can one fellow convince all the other Martians, and Mugs too, that we should be set free?"

"I don't know how, Don. But I have a hunch that Mahkee can do it if anyone can."

Mahkee was with the men many times during the next few days. He stared at them for hours and at their strange chess set. Every time he came, the men were hopeful that he would bring some news, but he told nothing. He acted as if their release had never been discussed.

"Why don't we ask him if he has done anything," Jack suggested. The waiting was becoming unbearable to him. "I think he's forgotten all about the *Lodestar*."

"I think not, Jack. He may resent being questioned. There is nothing we can do but wait; if we ask him we may destroy the confidence we have built."

It was difficult for Jack to see Dr. Shallot's reasoning, but this was no time to question his judgment. So what seemed to be two more days went by, with Mahkee coming, staying a few hours, and then leaving, without having said a single word.

On the third day Mahkee came; and, instead of taking his usual position beside Dr. Shallot, he stood in the doorway and beckoned, while he made strange sounds.

Dr. Shallot listened carefully. "Jack, Don," he said excitedly, "this it it. Mahkee says we're to come with him."

"Good old Mahkee," said Mr. Warick as he struggled to his feet. "Looks as if he didn't forget us after all."

Dr. Shallot and Jack picked up the chess set. "*Lodestar,* here we come," Jack said happily as he swung the jacket over his friend's shoulder.

Once more they moved along the corridor. They could move much faster now without tiring because their bodies were more used to the thin air. They were in gay spirits, the brightest in a long time. There was a swagger and lightness in their strides.

"He certainly keeps things to himself," said Mr. Warick to no one in particular. And to Dr. Shallot, who had turned toward him, he added, "Let's ask him where we're going. There shouldn't be any harm in that."

"All right. I'll ask him."

When Mahkee answered Dr. Shallot, his face showed his disappointment. It was unnecessary to ask him what had been said.

"This is no escape, or even another hearing," he reported. "We're going to visit the pneumatics plant." Their faces fell, so he added quickly, "Don't show your disappointment. Try to be enthusiastic, for we don't want to hurt Mahkee's feelings. Keep your eyes wide open, and maybe we'll find a way of getting out of here."

It seemed wise to talk less and observe more, so the procession moved along with no further talk. It was a glum group that halted before the vaultlike doors of the pneumatics and atmosphere plant.

But once they were inside the plant they forgot their disappointment. They were finding here more fascinating answers to their questions about the Martian way of life. When they stepped through the door, they entered a room whose walls were exactly like those of their prison room; but the room was much larger. It was about the size of a basketball floor, and forty or fifty feet high. They could see only pipes and tanks and pumps, all seemingly arranged in a haphazard manner.

Mahkee moved to the far left of the plant, the whole of which was brightly lighted by a brilliant glow that spread from the ceiling.

The men followed him and moved halfway along the length of the room until they came to a hole two feet square in the wall. A continuous belt was moving through this hole, carrying the same red powder that covered the surface of the planet. The powder was emptied into a vertically moving chain of buckets that carried it to the ceiling, where it was dumped into a large metal tank.

As they had found out by their analyses aboard the *Lodestar,* the red powder was an oxide, or rather a combination of many oxides. It was rich in iron and mercury, and contained numerous other substances in smaller amounts. The Martians were engaged in gathering this powder and breaking it down into the elements of which it was made.

The powder was pushed onto the endless belt by machines like a bulldozer that were radio controlled. A Martian sat in a transparent blister on the surface. Before him was a series of several banks of push buttons. Each bank controlled a machine which shoved the red powder onto the belt. The belt extended at least a mile along the surface.

As the belt moved along, they noticed that the red powder was not evenly distributed, but was mounded at regular intervals. This was because the belt had to move through a pressure lock so the pressure inside the plant could not escape. As the belt entered the lock, its load was held back by squeezers that permitted only the belt to move through. When the powder had piled up, the inner gate closed and the outer gate opened. The belt then carried the powder within the pressure chamber. Once inside it, the outer gate closed and the inner one opened, permitting the powder to be carried within the plant. The opening and closing of the two locks, as well as the intermittent motion of the belt, were automatically controlled so everything went along smoothly.

When Jack saw this belt, he thought, "Here's an escape. If we could only get this thing reversed, it would carry us out of here."

The large tank into which the powder was dumped was a centrifuge that separated the various oxides, such as iron, lead, and mercuric. Each oxide was then shunted into a catalytic tank where the oxygen was freed by chemical action, and by heating. The metals thus liberated went to the bottom of the tanks.

The free gas was collected and piped into another cylindrical tank where it liquefied immediately. The men were amazed to see this happen, for they knew that on earth great pressures were needed to change a gas into a liquid. The Martians had found an easier way of bringing about this change, and, as the men later found out, the Martian oxygen was a peculiar isotope of the element, one unknown upon earth. By liquefying the gas, they could store a vast amount in a relatively small space. The tank into which the oxygen was going, and in which it was being changed to a liquid, contained enough oxygen to make up millions of cubic feet when changed to a gas.

An adjacent tank contained nitrogen which was recovered from waste gases. These two liquefied gases entered large pipes where they were allowed to evaporate. The pipes carried the gases from the tanks to a mixing valve where they were combined in a ratio of five parts of nitrogen to one of oxygen. This mixture entered massive blowers that spread the gases throughout the Martian domain. The gases were at a pressure of only twenty-two inches.

The crew were used to a pressure of thirty inches, as are all earth people. This difference in pressure, together with the fact that the air contained less oxygen than that usually breathed, explained why the men had been tiring so rapidly.

In the atmosphere plant, as elsewhere on Mars, nothing went to waste. Everything that could be utilized was conserved. The atmosphere was kept circulating by the master pumps that the men saw in the plant and by a series of lesser pumps, each located strategically.

Eventually all the air passed through analyzing and separating devices. The nitrogen in the air, the amount of which was substantially the same as when it left the plant, went into the tank for that gas, and the oxygen was returned to its tank. The returned air contained a considerable amount of carbon dioxide, which is a waste product of animals. This gas was conducted into a third reservoir where it was solidified, making dry ice. The reservoir was never completely filled. This left a space above the solid material that contained carbon dioxide gas. Pumps pushed this gas through pipes to the various farms where the plants used it as a raw material in the manufacture of food.

The handling of water, which was a rare substance on Mars, and yet vital to life itself, was part of the work carried on by the atmosphere plant. Most of the water used by the Martians, as well as that in the tanks that fed the plants, was obtained from the small amount in the outside atmosphere and from the minute amounts in the red powder that covered the surface. An almost negligible amount was made by combining oxygen and hydrogen.

As the red powder was carried along the continuous belt to the separation tanks where the oxygen was obtained, the belt passed through an evaporator where every bit of water was removed. When the powder left the device, every grain of it was bone dry. It looked dry when it went in; but actually there were several drops in each ten pounds. The water thus collected was condensed, purified, and stored in covered reservoirs.

The daily supplies were doled out with precision. Each Martian received not one more drop than was absolutely essential for the maintenance of life. All waste water was carefully processed, purified by distillation, and conducted back to the reservoir.

When they saw how hard it was for the Martians to obtain water, the men easily understood why they had been given such a limited amount.

The more they learned about the Martian way of life, the more the crew respected their captors' ingenuity. The

Martians were performing, as an everyday matter, feats which people on earth had thought impossible. Even though this excursion had brought the crew no nearer escape, they were grateful to Mahkee for showing them the intricate workings of the Martian community.

12. AHMON, THE OLD ONE

TWO DAYS went by before Mahkee was seen again. Dr. Shallot spent much of this time recording the observations the crew had made. He wrote with great care in order to extend the limited supply of paper as far as possible. There was much to say, and little space in which to say it.

In the middle of what they reckoned was the second day after the excursion to the pneumatics plant, Mahkee came once more. He entered without making the slightest sound and stood motionless just within the doorway. Dr. Shallot stopped writing and walked slowly toward Mahkee. The two communicated together for several minutes in low tones and with many gestures.

Jack said quietly to Mr. Warick, "Maybe this is the good news we've been waiting for."

"Maybe so," answered Mr. Warick, while he kept his

eyes on Mahkee. "I believe that puckish fellow is excited
for once. He doesn't show anything at all; but I think his
blood is flowing faster than it usually does."

Dr. Shallot pushed his memo pad into his shirt pocket
and strode toward Jack and Don. "We're going somewhere with Mahkee. It's not anything like the places we've
been. From what he says I think we're going a long way
this time, but where we'll end up I don't know. He can't
seem to find any words to tell me."

"Maybe we're going to the *Lodestar*," Don suggested
hopefully.

"Let's hope so," said the doctor. "But we have no way
of knowing. All we can do is hope for the best. All set?"

Once more the procession of four moved along the
dimly lighted corridor with Mahkee in the lead, maintain-
ing a smooth, effortless walk with his short, spindly legs.
The ease with which he moved never ceased to amaze
them. His huge head seemed to be an unbearably top-
heavy burden for so small a body, but his grace was un-
deniable.

They walked slowly along the corridor for a long time,
past the doors that led into the farm and the atmosphere
plant. On and on they walked, past the door that led to
the great auditorium where they had been sentenced. Mr.
Warick winced as he passed it.

When they peered ahead, they could see nothing, for

the light was dim, and what light there was faded into darkness twenty or thirty feet from them. Farther and farther they walked, yet there was no change. The corridor was the same, and always there was nothing ahead but darkness. Jack looked back, and the picture was no different: dim light fading into blackness rapidly. He did not know whether the tunnel was straight or crooked, for his outlook was too limited.

The corridor came to an end abruptly, and branched to the right and left, making a *T* intersection. With no hesitation, Mahkee took the right-hand corridor. This corridor was precisely the same as the other one. There were three more such intersections, and they took the left, right, and left turns in that order.

The men had been doing little talking. Walking itself required too much exertion in the rarefied atmosphere, even though they had become partially adapted to it. But after they had been walking what seemed to Jack a very long time, he asked Dr. Shallot, "How long have we been on this march?"

Dr. Shallot held his watch close to his eyes so he could see it in the dim light. "Hm, not as long as I thought. Only two and a half hours."

"Is that all?" asked Jack incredulously. "It seems to me we've been walking for days."

"The surroundings make it seem longer. We walk and

walk and walk, and everything is precisely the same as it was when we began."

"Except that I'm a lot more tired," put in Mr. Warick. And then he added, "But tired or not, I'm going to keep close to Mahkee. I'm so mixed up I could never find my way back again."

A short time later Mahkee stopped before a door, sent out a radio signal, and the door raised quickly and silently. Mahkee stepped through, and the men followed. The room they entered was small and barren of furnishings. The light was dim, but there was enough for the men to see the inevitable four rock walls.

Was this a new prison cell? they wondered. Mr. Warick suspected this when Mahkee left them, and he was convinced of it when the door slid down, cutting them off completely and sealing them into a vault of solid rock.

"Well," he said as he stretched out on the floor and watched the door close, "that's that. I guess we're going from bad to worse. In the other cell they left the door open. Here they close it tight."

"Mahkee is returning, Don," said Dr. Shallot as he too stretched on the floor to rest his weary muscles. "He's gone for some food."

Mahkee returned, as Dr. Shallot had said he would. And he brought with him a group of Martians carrying a bountiful display of food and water. They placed the trays on the floor and left immediately.

But Mahkee stayed and ate with the men, although he sat off to one side. Jack noticed that he ate not one-tenth the amount that each of them consumed. When Mahkee finished eating, he lay down, or rather he laid down his massive head. The crew lay down also, and their exhaustion was so great that sleep came quickly.

The next day they walked through corridors exactly the same as those through which they had come. So far as they could tell, they might have been walking back in the direction they had come, for they had lost their bearings completely.

But in a few hours the corridor changed. The ceiling shortened. Up to this time the tunnel had been high enough for everyone to walk erect, with about four inches of head room. But now they were forced to stoop. They walked in a half crouch for an hour. It seemed to them that their backs would break and their legs would buckle under them.

"What a punishment," thought Jack. "I thought the duck waddle we used in football practice was bad. This is a hundred times worse."

"Why don't we stop a while?" asked Mr. Warick. "My back is about to break. If I stay crouched like this much longer, I'll be stooped the rest of my life."

For five days the journey continued. The men walked in this same wearisome crouch for miles and miles through the maze of underground corridors and lay down on the stone floor to rest at night. On the sixth day of the journey, Mahkee stopped before a door that was decorated elaborately with carvings that seemed to the tired men to be colored with ancient dyes. They watched Mahkee as he hesitated in front of the door.

He made no move to touch it or open it in any way. Instead he swung around his antenna eye until it was directly opposite the center of a series of concentric circles. To Jack he seemed to be looking inside through a peephole in the door.

The men took advantage of the break in their travels and sat on their haunches directly behind Mahkee. They dared not lie down, however much they wished to, for they wanted to be alert and ready for whatever might happen.

"This must be something special," said Mr. Warick. "It's the first door we've seen decorated. And if you ask me, our friend Mahkee is scared. Maybe it's a torture chamber, or the place of execution."

"It's special, all right," said Dr. Shallot. "But I don't think it can be a torture chamber. I don't think that sort of treatment would enter their heads." As he spoke, he opened his notebook and sketched the design on the door.

"I wouldn't agree with that," said Jack. "Walking through those low tunnels was torture."

"True enough," said Dr. Shallot as he rested his hand on his hip and arched his back. He looked at Mahkee and added, "Did you ever see him act so queerly? I wonder what's going on in there."

Mahkee moved from the door and motioned the doctor to look. Dr. Shallot rose to his knees so his eyes were level with the lens that formed the peephole, and gazed through it.

Jack could hardly wait for his turn. But when it came the sight was worth the wait.

He saw a large circular room, heavily draped with soft-looking fabrics of many pastel colors that blended with each other. There were soft yellows, pinks, greens, blues, and lavenders. He could not be sure if the fabrics themselves were colored, or if the colors and their blending were produced by an ingenious method of artificial lighting. He was soothed by its beauty. The fabrics, which were the first he had seen on the planet, were gathered at the center and raised to the ceiling so the effect was as though one were looking into the interior of a fabulous circus tent. The place appeared to be completely silent.

Martians squatted at regular intervals around the outside of the circle. Or were they Martians? At first they looked like Mahkee, but when he looked more closely

Jack could see that they were different. It was not their
bodies, for they were no heavier than Mahkee; nor their
antennae, because these looked the same. It was their
faces, and their postures. Age was the difference. They
held up their heads with great difficulty, and their eyes
were rheumy and weak, like those of the very old. Each
of the figures was facing the center of the room, either
gazing intently or staring blankly, but always reverently.

At the center of the room was the oldest creature Jack
had ever seen. He was stretched out on a pallet and his
head was raised slightly from the velvet-covered floor.
The head was strangely young in comparison with the
withered body. This creature was Ahmon, who was called
"the Old One."

As Jack watched him through the peephole, the Martian who was sitting nearest to the door rose to his feet
effortlessly and came toward them. He, too, seemed to
Jack to be old—very old.

The door rose soundlessly, and a clean fresh odor like
that of newly laundered linen surrounded the men. The
circle of Martians funneled them as they moved toward
the pallet. They felt humble and uncertain.

Ahmon, who lay before them motionless except for the
antenna eye that moved about vigorously, was at least a
thousand years old, and it was thought that he could live
as many years more. At first the men could not believe

that anyone could be that old; but it was easier to under-stand after they heard his story. Here it is, told through Mahkee and interpreted by Dr. Shallot:

Not many centuries ago Mars was a flourishing planet with a vast population. In the tropics only a relatively small area was inhabited; the great mass of Martians lived in the temperate areas and were divided into two groups: the upper and the lower sections. Ahmon was the long-acknowledged coordinator, or supreme ruler, of the two groups. Mugs was the leader of the upper section. The lower section had gone into oblivion. At that time the atmosphere around the planet was more dense, and the heat that was received from the sun could not escape easily; therefore the planet remained warm, although its mean temperature never reached that of earth.

The Martians in the northern hemisphere reached a very high degree of civilization. They learned to supply the body with the exact amounts of various needed chem-icals. They learned how to destroy and control bacteria, making it possible for them to wipe out all diseases caused by these organisms. And they had reached a level of civ-ilization that caused them to frown upon unnecessary labor, anxieties and worries. This made them healthier. They also learned how to replace or repair virtually every organ of the body. Since they could do these things, the Martians lived very long lives.

It was not uncommon for individuals to live for three or four hundred years, and in some rare cases, or when they were given special attention as in the case of Ahmon, they lived much longer than this. Ahmon was the last survivor of the great calamity that had happened seven hundred years ago, and which was to bring about the eventual destruction of the Martian civilization. His great age and vast knowledge accounted for the respect that the population tendered him. Mugs was a governor under Ahmon's command. Like the other Martians, Mugs was loyal to Ahmon, although he did not always agree with his decisions completely. This disagreement was the cause of much of the discomfort of the crew, and also their near calamity.

When the Martian civilization was at its peak, a group of researchers devised a powerful ejector that was able to send small rocketlike projectiles into space. Although man-carrying rockets were never developed, a plan for colonizing other parts of the universe was made. Various seeds, spores, and living primary cells were placed in these tiny rockets, or pellets, and ejected into space. If the pellets struck a solid surface, they would burst open and the contents would be spread over the surface. If they fell on a spot where conditions were favorable, various forms of life would evolve. Ahmon was convinced that the three men from the *Lodestar* were derived from these primary cells. Since he believed that they came from these cells, he assumed that the members of the crew were related to him and to all the other people of Mars.

Although the Martians were geniuses in biological and chemical matters, they—or at least some of them—were bunglers in the field of practical nuclear physics. A group of Martians had done research in nuclear physics, trying to release from the nucleus of the atom the energy they believed to be locked within it. They succeeded in this venture. But the results were far from the beneficial ones they anticipated, for their questionable success brought about the present undesirable condition of the people, and would bring about the obliteration of life on the planet eventually.

The nuclear experiments had been performed in the southern hemisphere. When the energy was released, a chain reaction was set up which could not be controlled and which destroyed all the life existing in that area. The radiation from the reaction spread throughout the globe and affected every Martian alive at that time, as well as those who were still unborn. The genes, which are the agents of inheritance, were strongly affected. Although no change was noticeable in the first generation, a gradual deterioration of the organs of reproduction took place until no Martian could bear young. This occurred in the third generation after the nuclear reaction. No child had been born in the past four hundred years. The Martians were destined for extinction, for there was no way of replacing those who died. The process would be a long one, since life could be prolonged, but the ultimate finish was inevitable.

This explained why the crew had been so well cared for. Life was revered throughout the planet and, in fact, it was questionable if the Martians now living realized that a life could be taken by violence.

When the chain reaction was set off, the oxygen of the atmosphere began to combine with the various substances of the surface. This reduced to an alarming degree the amount of free, usable oxygen. Apparently the nuclear reaction created a catalytic agent that helped this oxidation process to occur more rapidly than it would have normally.

It was not long before chemists noted the reduction of oxygen in the atmosphere. A careful check was made of the rate of reduction, and it was found to be proceeding with alarming speed. The Martians knew immediately that they were faced with extinction if they did not act at once and with great haste, for they could not live in their atmosphere if the oxygen supply continued to decline. It was then that the underground installations were made, so that they could control the air supply as well as regulate temperature and pressure.

Some of the Martians had trained themselves to go out into the free air, but they could do this only after an adjustment period. Even then they could remain outside for only a short interval.

Ahmon spoke in a whisper to Mahkee. His voice was so weak that often the men could not hear him. Now that he had spoken, Ahmon asked innumerable questions, most of which were difficult, if not impossible to answer.

He cross-examined them to see if their beginnings would support his belief that the men were derived from the pellets that had been shot out from his own planet. Ahmon wanted to know how long the earth had existed, when life began upon the earth, where it came from, and how.

These were questions that could not be answered, and the doctor told him so, although earth people could and did make guesses about the answers.

"At last you know," Ahmon said with great dignity. "You have come a long way to learn these answers. But I have spoken, and you need wonder no longer. You are derived from the primary cells that were in our colonizing pellets. You are descended from the people of Mars."

Dr. Shallot did not argue the point through Mahkee, for it would have done him no good to antagonize the Old One.

Ahmon said that his countrymen knew little about

space, about the stars, and about the place called earth, although much was known about these things by Ahmon. The crew had been brought before him so he could check their story and thus help the people decide if they had been truthful and were on their planet for peaceful purposes or if they were bent on destruction—as Mugs had told them.

Ahmon's eyes closed slowly and his head sagged as a puppet's does when the supporting string is broken. The two attendants, who had been standing close by, sprang to his side and settled him comfortably. Ahmon had finished; the audience was ended.

Mahkee led the way back through the ornate door and to the room the crew had occupied the previous night. There the men fell asleep from exhaustion and frayed nerves. The next day they were ushered into Ahmon's chamber once more. As usual the Martians showed no sign of their feelings, so the men had no inkling of what was to happen.

They were amazed to see Ahmon looking so well. The day before he looked as though he might never recover from the collapse, and now he appeared just as fresh as when the men first saw him. He was the Martian supreme ruler, and as such all of the science of the medical men was at his disposal. They had done well by him. He spoke to Mahkee with new vigor.

Ahmon had mulled over the interview at length. He remembered about earth, and so the story that the *Lodestar* had come from there did not sound fantastic to him. He believed therefore that the crew were ambassadors of good will, and that their mission was of great importance for the future of life in the solar system. He had already dispatched radio messages throughout the land saying that the men were to be treated as honored guests, that they were to be given whatever they desired in the way of provisions, equipment, and information. He then wished them good fortune, and ended the audience.

"Wow," Jack exploded as soon as they were out in the corridor, "*Lodestar*, here we come."

13. MUGS AGAIN

THE HAPPINESS that filled their hearts when they heard the good news lightened their feet on the return journey. Dr. Shallot pushed and prodded Mahkee, trying to make him move faster. He was not speeded up easily, but after many unsuccessful attempts he did move a bit faster, and the crew were back in their quarters after only three sleeps.

When they arrived in their room, Mahkee left, saying he would return shortly. The men were so exhausted, they could not sleep. But even if they had been physically able to sleep, mentally they would have been unable to do so, for their minds were full of speculation about what was going to happen next.

News travels fast. This was as true on Mars as on earth. Mahkee had not been gone an hour when visitors arrived. Fourteen Martians entered the room in a formal procession, arranged themselves in a semicircle around the men, and gave no clue at all to their intentions. One of the men moved within the group, stepping forward as a spokesman might whose pleasure it was to congratulate the men and extend their courtesy. But that was not his purpose.

The Martian who stepped ahead of the group was Mugs, the judge who had tried the crew and sentenced them. He spoke in a high-pitched, sing-song monotone. Jack and Mr. Warick could not understand a single sound that he made. At intervals a low murmur of approval sifted through the Martians who stood like statues behind their ruler. Jack's muscles were tensed and alert to whatever might happen. He looked out of the corner of his eye at Dr. Shallot, who was trying to recognize the few sounds he knew of the Martian language. It was obvious from his expression that the words were not happy ones.

Mugs made it clear enough why he had paid the crew a visit, the first since their capture and sentencing.

He, Mugs, was the ruler of the Martians, and his word was law. The men had been given a trial before the assembled people and it had been decided that they were dangerous to the peace and well-being of the planet. As ruler of the Martians he had decreed that the crew were to be held captive forever. And that was the way it would be. There would be no release, no change in the original sentence.

Mugs had spoken. He stepped back into the group; and, as quietly as it had come, the procession moved out of the room, into the hallway, and out of sight.

This was real trouble. It had been obvious at the gathering in the main hall that Mugs had a strong hold on the populace. Was their good fortune to die so quickly? And what about Ahmon? Were his words nothing? Was he not the supreme ruler of the Martian people? What was to be done about Mugs and his opposition? When Mahkee came again the doctor plied him with these questions.

Mahkee said that it was true that Ahmon was the supreme ruler; but it was also true that Mugs was the person who made the laws and passed sentences. It was true that the words of Ahmon were the final authority, even beyond Mugs'. But Mahkee could not recall any time when Ahmon had spoken before, and certainly no time when his word had opposed that of Mugs. The people knew Mugs because he lived among them, and so they were loyal to him. They knew Ahmon too, but more as a legend than as a real person. They held him in great respect and awe. Now that the orders of Mugs and Ahmon conflicted, the people were very upset. They knew and liked Mugs, and believed in him; but they respected and revered Ahmon and felt that what he directed was all-wise. Mahkee assured the crew that most of the people supported Ahmon and felt that the men should be released. But Mugs had a group banded about him who were just as sure that the crew should not be released because they firmly believed that their purpose was to bring about the immediate and complete destruction of the Martian people.

"Well," said Jack, "now what? I had visions of walking out of here with their blessings."

"Maybe we shall yet," said Dr. Shallot as he rubbed his brow. "At least we know where we stand. We know Mugs' intentions and we can prepare to meet him on his own terms."

"Let's get our pressure suits," suggested Mr. Warick with determination, "and make a try for it right now. I'll bet we can get out of here with Mahkee's help. One thing is sure, we'll never know until we try."

"Golly," said Jack, "the pressure suits! I hope Mugs hasn't got them. He'd ruin them."

Dr. Shallot spoke to Mahkee about the suits, but his words and descriptive actions made no impression. However, after he ran his hands up and down his body to show the size of the torso and leg sections, Mahkee suddenly left. He returned shortly with several helpers, each of whom was carrying various sections of the suits.

The suits were intact and looked as though they had not been tampered with in any way. The men were becoming more excited with each minute that passed. Then

Mr. Warick, who was checking the gauges on the air tanks, dashed their spirits.

"Oh, oh," he said as he tapped the indicators, "there's no air in the reserve tanks. There's not enough here to take us back to the ship even if we ran all the way, and no one could run in one of these things."

Dr. Shallot and Jack looked at the gauges. They tapped and jiggled them, hoping that they were jammed. But not one of them budged. The air supply would last six minutes, and no longer. This was barely enough time to reach ground level. Apparently the valves had been opened, either accidentally or intentionally.

"Hmm," mused the doctor, "I wonder—"

"What, Dr. Shallot," Jack said impatiently, "what are you thinking?"

"I was wondering if we could get into the atmosphere plant. All we need is a pressure pump, then we can fill the tanks."

"A pump will do it if we can get the air. But these fellows don't have any to spare. Every bit they have comes from that processed powder."

"All we can do is try, Jack. I'll see if Mahkee will take me to the plant."

Mahkee agreed to take his mustached friend to the atmosphere plant and they set out, taking the three tanks with them. Mr. Warick and Jack remained behind to protect the pressure suits. Now that they knew there were enemies who were determined to prevent their escape, they had to take every precaution.

An hour dragged by, and then another before Dr. Shallot returned. He had been successful, for the filled tanks were carried in by Martians who had offered their aid. He had met no opposition at all, for like most of the others, the Martians at the pneumatics plant were anxious to co-operate, although they were reluctant to part with their precious air. This was a good sign.

Once the tanks were filled with air, they decided to leave at once. If all went well and Mugs did not interfere with their plans, the crew wanted to return to the Martian underground once they had left, for there was a great deal of information they wanted to get about the Martian way of life. They wished to learn why the Martians lived in large groups rather than in small family units as the earth people did.

Dr. Shallot told Mahkee of this desire, and the two of them made an arrangement so the crew could move back and forth between the *Lodestar* and the underground. The men put on their pressure suits, except for the head globes and set out toward the pit, with Mahkee leading the way. Bulky as they were, the suits felt good to them, for they meant release from the long imprisonment.

Jack expected Mugs and his followers to swarm over

them at any moment. Not a sound could be heard. Dr. Shallot and Mr. Warick were keeping a close watch both in front and in back of them. Mahkee seemed oblivious to the danger that the men felt all about them, for he walked ahead slowly in his customary rolling stride.

They came to a door, not in any way different from those they had gone through previously. Mahkee gave a signal and it rose.

They found themselves in a room about ten feet square, at one end of which was a strong-looking door with a series of panels built into it. The panels alternately glowed and dimmed as if they were alive and pulsating. This was a precautionary measure to make the door appear different from the others and to prevent the accidental opening of it.

Mahkee said a few singsong words to Dr. Shallot. The men put on their head globes and opened the air valves. From now on gestures would be their only means of conversation, for the radio batteries had given out during the long storage.

This must be the pressure lock, thought Jack. He would have said it had his radio been working. That glowing door must lead to the outside.

When the valves had been opened, Mahkee sent out a signal and the door went up. Before them was a roofless pit that looked exactly like the one they had entered so long ago. They gazed up and saw light, natural light that was blinding even at the bottom of the pit. They closed their eyes tightly, and then opened them a little to admit only a small amount of the intense light.

They were outside.

The door closed quickly, for Mahkee had not been prepared to withstand the low outside pressure. Jack looked at Dr. Shallot and Mr. Warick with consternation. He was trying to say, "Where's Mugs? I thought he was going to keep us from getting to the *Lodestar*."

It was apparent that they understood, for Jack's look was answered by questioning shrugs of their shoulders.

The men climbed the long vertical ladder that led to the surface. As their heads rose above ground level they could see the *Lodestar* standing majestically in the cold sunlight, her sleek, silver nose pointing defiantly into the reaches of space. Jack's eyes filled and his throat choked, for she was a welcome and beautiful sight.

The men were spellbound by the space about them. For weeks they had been limited by the walls of the underground. Seeing endless space was as soothing and refreshing as a cool dip on a hot, muggy day.

Jack shuffled his feet in the dull red powder and reached down to run his fingers through it, as he used to when he went swimming in the rolling surf at the seashore. Dr. Shallot was the first to recover from the spell cast upon the crew by the broad daylight. He pushed through the powder in a straight line toward the *Lodestar*. Since talk was impossible, he signaled the others to follow him.

Jack was so anxious to get there that he moved ahead, but he tired quickly because the space suit hampered his motions.

In spite of the powdery surface and the discomfort of the suits, the men found themselves walking faster and faster as they neared the ship. They kept their eyes glued to it. Now they could see the small vents at the nose where the reverse jets had melted out the plates. The skin shone with the same rich luster it had always had. Now they could see that the red dust had drifted about the stilts, but the stilts themselves looked perfect.

Jack was in the lead as they approached the first stilt. He stared at it with horror. He ran up and touched his hand to it. Great flakes of rust fell into his hand, and even as he looked at it, more flakes were forming. This was Mugs' way of thwarting their escape. If the men could not enter their ship again, they would have to return to the underground or perish.

Don Warick ran to another stilt and found that this one was rusting also.

Dr. Shallot went to the ladder that approached the escape hatch. When he put his weight on a rung to pull himself up, the rung broke off in his hand and he fell on his back. He struggled to right himself and then tried the ladder again. By putting his weight on the edge of the rungs he was able to make his way to the escape hatch. He reached frantically for the manual latch of the door. Part of it broke off in his hand as he attempted to turn it. He tried again and the door swung open. He motioned Jack and Mr. Warick, who were running toward the ladder, to wait for him, and then pulled himself inside the ship.

"If Mugs has been inside," thought Jack, "everything will be ruined. If the controls are gone we'll never get the ship off the ground."

In a few minutes Dr. Shallot lowered himself out of the ship. He had a small drum of acid slung over his shoulder. He moved rapidly from one stilt to another, dousing them and the escape hatch with the acid, hoping that this would neutralize whatever substance Mugs had put on the metal parts.

The rusting action slowed down immediately. Then he motioned the others to follow him into the ship. When they looked around, they found that everything was intact. Mugs had not found the controls for the hatch and so had been unable to enter.

"We were lucky we got here when we did," said Dr. Shallot as soon as they had removed their globes. "A few more days and the stilts would have collapsed. If that happened we'd be marooned here for a long time, maybe for the rest of our lives."

"Everything was going too smoothly," said Mr. Warick. "I thought we were going to be attacked any moment when we were moving along the corridor. When no one bothered us I was more nervous. If something's going to happen I'd rather have it over with than go on wondering about it."

And then he patted the bulkhead affectionately.

"Well," he said, "Mugs or no Mugs. I give three cheers for the *Lodestar*. And right here and now I promise never to get tired of her again."

"Just like home, isn't it," said Jack as he settled into one of the chairs. "And it's just as warm and snug as the day we left it."

"The gauges are working perfectly," said Dr. Shallot as he switched on one control after another. "And the clock, too. The second hand is still whirling around." He took out his notebook where he had been keeping track of the days. "And look at this," he said. "I'm only two days off. The automatic calendar reads September eighteenth and I have today as the sixteenth."

"That's not bad at all," said Mr. Warick. "We probably missed those two when we were going to see Ahmon."

"That could be," said Dr. Shallot as he continued checking. "How's the food and water supply, Don?"

Mr. Warick checked these and found everything in good order. He then prepared to leave the ship to see if the corrosion had been stopped completely.

"While you're out there I'll rustle up something to eat," said Jack. "It seems to me that we haven't eaten for days and days."

Jack cooked a meal of dried meat, potato flakes, and powdered milk which was served after Don returned to report that the stilts were in fairly good condition and had not been dangerously weakened. The meal tasted good, to their surprise. While they were eating, they laid their plans.

"Let's get started back as soon as we can," suggested Mr. Warick between mouthfuls.

"We all agree to that, Don," said Dr. Shallot. "But we've lost a lot of research time, and there's much to do yet."

"I'd like to know how the Martians get their power," said Jack. "I've been wondering about that for a long time. Whatever it is, or however they get it, I haven't been able to figure out."

"And there are a good many other things we have to find out, too."

"Say, Doctor," said Mr. Warick seriously, "what are you going to do about that mustache of yours?"

"Well," said Dr. Shallot. He smiled as he stroked it. "This old mustache worked a miracle for us because it brought us Mahkee. Without him we would have learned nothing at all. I think it would be disloyal for me to shave it off, don't you?"

"Shave it off," said Mr. Warick who was aghast at the thought, "heavens no. I think it should be preserved in a museum."

"Later on we'll decide which museum, Don, but now we'd better figure out the jobs that have to be done."

The three men were in a gay mood, and they talked on and on, sometimes seriously and sometimes lightly.

It was decided that Jack and Dr. Shallot would visit the power plant if it could be arranged. Photographs would be made of this and other installations as far as time and film footage allowed. The provisions would be checked and brought up to peak wherever possible. They decided that the *Lodestar* was to take off in five days on her return journey.

The only black spot in all the planning was Mugs. The crew had had a taste of the methods that he would employ to stop them, and they were determined to be alert at all times. The ship would never be left unguarded.

After the business of eating was over, the men cleaned themselves thoroughly. The clothes they had been wearing were dirty and thin in places so they changed to clean, new outfits. The old suits were not washed, because the water could not be spared, even though most of it would be reclaimed. But they were stowed away, since no one could know if and when the old ones would be needed.

The men basked in the comfort of the ship. For weeks they had sat on nothing softer than solid rock. It was a pleasure to relax in their comfortable bucket seats. When they went to bed, Jack could not fall asleep on the foam mattress. It was too soft. But he convinced himself that he would get used to such luxury, so he lay upon it until sleep came.

Dr. Shallot and Jack left the *Lodestar* early the next morning, hoping they could persuade Mahkee to show them the Martian power plant. Mr. Warick was left behind to guard the *Lodestar* and also to make a detailed plan of procedure for the few days the crew would remain on this foreign planet.

To avoid a recurrence of disaster, they decided that the man left on the ship was not to leave it for any reason. If the men in the underground did not return, the man aboard was to wait for thirty days, no more and no less. After that time he was to attempt to take off the ship singlehanded. There was a slim chance that this could be done; but no matter how small the chance might be, it would be safer than would venturing into the underground to attempt a rescue of the other crew members.

"Let's hope this reception is more pleasant than the last one," said Dr. Shallot. The radios could be used again, for they had been supplied with fresh batteries.

"I keep wondering what Mugs will do next," said Jack as they pushed through the powdery surface. "Let's hope we don't meet him instead of Mahkee."

They equipped themselves the same as they had on previous trips. Dr. Shallot had a camera with him in addition to the usual apparatus.

At the pit, from which they had emerged the day before, Dr. Shallot went down the ladder first, and Jack followed him closely. They got to the bottom without mishap, pounded on the door, and waited. In a few minutes the door opened but no one was there.

"I guess they want us to go right in," Jack said as he watched the leader's face.

Dr. Shallot raised his eyebrows questioningly, and then said, "I guess so." He stepped through the doorway. "The greeting isn't overly social, but it's better than last time. First a mob swarms over us, and then there's no one at all to receive us."

After the two of them had passed through, the door closed quickly and silently. Jack turned as it reached the bottom. He would never be used to those automatic doors. There was another one immediately in front of them. A small panel opened in it.

"Apparently we're supposed to crawl through that," said Dr. Shallot. "You first, Jack."

The boy wiggled through the panel. As he straightened, Mahkee was standing before him in the erect posture that was typical of all Martians. Jack was sure it was Mahkee, although he could not say why he knew. It was not his appearance certainly, for he looked the same as all the other Martians—spindly, hair-covered body, and a large, white globe of a head surmounted with two antennae, one ending in a roving eye, the other in a brass radio aerial. It must have been the way in which he stood, or the appearance of the small piglike eyes that were set in his head. Nevertheless he was sure it was Mahkee, and not Mugs, as he had feared it might be. Once Dr. Shallot was inside, the two of them shut off their air valves and removed the head globes.

Mahkee agreed to take them to the power plant. The plant was overwhelming, not only because of its great size but also because of the ingenuity displayed in it. The Martians had harnessed the sun directly.

As they entered the plant, they heard a light, buzzing sound. Directly to the right of them was a master board of switches, dials, and controls that reminded Jack of the control panels he had seen in the atomic electric plants on earth. The area was about fifty feet high. The lower thirty feet contained what looked like sealed lockers connected by large ducts. The upper twenty feet contained a network of catwalks reached by a spiral staircase. The farther half of the upper section could not be seen very well from where Jack and Dr. Shallot were standing.

"Let's take off these suits," Jack suggested. "Then we can move around more easily."

"By all means," said Dr. Shallot. "I think they'll be safe here. If Mugs planned on damaging them he would have done so before now."

Mahkee was moving up the spiraling steps and the two followed him. As they moved upward, Jack looked ahead. He could see nothing, except that it was much brighter up there.

When they got to the top, Jack stared at the sight before him in admiration. Stretching the length of the installation was a section about twenty feet high and as many deep encased in a clear material that looked like plastic. A bank of lenses served as the ceiling. The entire section was sealed off from the rest of the plant, so a decreased pressure could be maintained inside it.

There was a battery of rotors in this compartment that were spinning around rapidly and almost magically, for nothing that was moving them could be seen. The rotors were made of four blades, each of which was a dull black on one side, and a bright silver on the other. They were mounted on a vertical shaft. As Jack looked more closely, he could see what made them move.

Sunlight was concentrated by the lenses and directed onto the blackened area of the blades. As the blades became heated, they warmed the air in contact with the blackened surfaces. The air expanded, and as it did it pushed the blade. This motion was picked up by the shaft. The action was much like that of instruments that were used on earth to detect radiant energy.

The shaft turned with very little force; but when the motion of all the rotors was transmitted to a gearlike chain, a powerful thrust was developed. This force was used to turn an electric generator, and the electricity was then used for power and light.

Since there was no weather on Mars, the sun could be depended on to shine every day. However, the installation was not effective after sunset, but the activities of the Martians ceased with the setting sun. The vital processes that had to continue were powered with current obtained from batteries of chemical cells.

Jack had noticed that there were no wires carrying current to different parts of the underground. He assumed that the wires must have been embedded in the rock, but he was to find that this was not the case. The Martians had developed wireless transmission of electric current by high-frequency signals and so no wires were required. The glowing light they had seen wherever they went, for example, was produced by high-frequency signals. These fell upon a mixture of mercury and fluorescent materials. The signals caused the mercury to activate the light producers and make the soft glow that lighted all parts of the Martian domain. Other electrical apparatus received energy by waves in a similar manner.

In addition to the power equipment, the upper level of the plant contained the heating apparatus. This was based on a simple idea: the fact that salts melt when they are heated and that the heat they take in will be released when the salt recrystallizes. The heat for melting the salts came from the sun. Although the amount of sunshine received by the planet was barely enough to raise its temperature to fifty degrees during midday, there was enough heat in the sunlight to keep the Martians warm when it was concentrated.

There were batteries of lenses that focused the light on dull black surfaces. These surfaces absorbed the heat. Air circulated through the space between these black panels and the lenses. The warmed air was carried to heat-storage bins which were actually cans of sodium sulfate. As the warmed air circulated around the bins, it melted the salts. Some of the warm air was pushed beyond these bins and entered the various corridors, rooms, and halls that comprised the living quarters of the Martian groups.

At night when no heat was supplied to the bins, the melted salts changed back to crystals. As they did so, they released heat. This heat was picked up by air that was moved past the bins by electrically driven fans.

The Martians had been keeping their quarters warm

in this way for hundreds of years, and there had been no appreciable breakdown in the salts, although a substance that prevented their forming into crusty layers had to be added occasionally.

Dr. Shallot took photographs constantly to help earth engineers duplicate such an installation.

As they climbed down to the lower level, Jack looked toward the far end of the plant where he could see a narrow passageway. Beyond this passageway was another identical battery of heat bins. The installation he was in was only one of a series, each of which operated independently of the others.

After saying their farewells through Mahkee to the six Martians who were operating the vast plant, Dr. Shallot and Jack made their way back to the *Lodestar*. Once inside their ship they were full of talk about what they had seen.

"And what about you?" they asked of Don Warick. "Did anything happen here?"

"Not a thing," said Mr. Warick. "I've been sorting, labeling, and cataloging these specimens, and I've made out a detailed schedule of work. Every time I checked through the sights, I could see nothing at all—absolutely nothing."

14. FAREWELL TO MARS

THE NEXT days were busy ones, for extensive explorations of the surface of the planet were made to collect samples of rock and mineral deposits; temperature and pressure data were obtained; and their experiences had to be recorded. The days were anxious ones, too, for uncertainty about their security and what Mugs might do to stop them bothered the crew.

They were undisturbed, however, until a day when Jack was left to guard the ship. Mr. Warick and Dr. Shallot had gone into the underground to take pictures of the Martians as they went about their various chores. Jack was busy labeling plant specimens. At regular intervals he went to the peep sight. The spectacle before him was as lifeless as it would have been were he on the moon, instead of on a planet where there were multitudes of living creatures.

But one time when Jack looked he saw something moving. His spine prickled for he could see that the moving objects were Martians, and he feared that they might be Mugs' men. They moved closer and closer on their spindly legs. Because of the distance, their bodies were indistinct, and only their heads could be seen. They looked like six huge white balls, being moved by some magical power.

"Why are they moving so slowly?" he thought. He knew that the Martians had to go through a pressure-reducing compartment before they could venture outside, and that once they were outside they had to move slowly to conserve their energy. But they were moving much more slowly than necessary.

He did not wonder long for he could soon see that the Martians were divided into three pairs, and each pair had a juglike container slung between them. Their slow struggling movements indicated that the loads were heavy, and they could move only with great effort. As they came closer to the ship, a pair headed toward each of the stabilizing stilts.

"They're going to cover the stilts with that rust accelerator," Jack said aloud.

His mind raced to find something that he could do to stop them. He knew that it would be foolish to venture out of the ship because they could swamp him in hand-to-hand fighting. There were six of them and he was alone. And he could not fire upon them, for that might bring tragic retaliation from the Martians, and Dr. Shallot and Mr. Warick were still underground.

Sweat was breaking out on his forehead, for he could think of nothing to stop them, and the Martians were moving forward steadily. Suddenly a plan occurred to him. He moved from the peep sight to the control panel, and eased the lever for the steering jets. He moved the lever to the low position and then rushed back to the sight.

Mugs and his crew had not reached the stilts, but they had dropped their heavy loads and were walking as rapidly as they could from the ship, for no Martian could actually run. The blast of hot gases that issued from the *Lodestar* was too much for them. They gathered at a distance from the ship, hesitated for a time as though they were conferring, and then moved away at their slow rolling pace.

Jack shut down the jets and breathed a sigh of relief. The plan had worked. He did no more classifying that day but kept a close watch through the peep sight to see if Mugs would return.

In another hour he saw Dr. Shallot and Mr. Warick in the distance, moving toward the *Lodestar*. He spoke to them over the radio. "Be careful as you near the ship. It may be warm."

"What's the matter?" asked Dr. Shallot. "Your voice sounds strained."

"Everything's all right," answered Jack, "but we had a few visitors a while ago."

He continued to talk to Dr. Shallot and Mr. Warick while they were entering the ship. When they were inside, he told them the details of what had happened. Then Dr. Shallot announced his decision.

"Men," he said, "I suggest that we make ready to take off. Mugs is persistent. I think we've not seen the last of him, and the sooner we're away from here, the safer we'll be."

There were no opposing votes, and the take-off preparations were started immediately. But, as Dr. Shallot had prophesied, the crew had not seen the last of Mugs.

News of Mugs' attempts to sabotage the *Lodestar* spread throughout the Martian realm. The people were incensed over his actions and demanded that something be done. This was an unprecedented event, and called for the trial of their leader. With their customary ingenuity and dispatch the Martians tried Mugs, found him guilty of subversive actions, and so banned him. This meant that he would be unable to associate with any Martian except one. It was this Martian's responsibility to make Mugs uncomfortable and miserable. Since

Mahkee was one of the strongest prosecutors of Mugs, it was decided that Mahkee was the one who should punish the offender.

Immediately after the trial Mugs implored Mahkee to aid him. Anything would be better than banishment, he said. Even death would be better than life in exile.

Mahkee didn't enjoy being a prosecutor any more than Mugs liked being a sentenced criminal. He had an idea for a solution which he carried out the next day.

The *Lodestar* was feverish with the excitement of the take-off, but even so, vigilance was maintained. Mr. Warick was checking through the sight when he exclaimed suddenly, "I'll be doggoned, Doctor, you were right. Here they come again."

He continued to look through the sight.

"I can make out only two of them," he said, "and they don't have a thing with them." As he moved from the sight, he said, "Here, take a look. See what you think."

Dr. Shallot stared for a few minutes.

"All I can see is the whiteness of those great heads of theirs," he said, "but I have a hunch one of them is Mahkee."

As he spoke, he moved away from the sight. "I'm going out to meet him," he said. "Maybe he's in trouble."

Mr. Warick and Don tried to dissuade him but he was

determined. He put on his pressure suit and dropped down to the surface.

The two figures came closer and closer to the ship. Jack watched them until they moved directly beneath the ship to the spot where the doctor was standing. Now they could not be seen, and all that he and Don could do was wonder what was going on.

After a few minutes Dr. Shallot's voice came over the radio.

"Prepare to take in these two fellows," he directed.

"Who are they?" asked Don.

"One is Mahkee," he said, "and the other one is Mugs. I can't understand exactly what they want, but I believe they want to get inside the ship. Keep an eye on them as they come through."

When they were inside the ship Mahkee told Dr. Shallot all about the events that had taken place: the trial, the sentence, and the appointment of Mahkee as prosecutor—a mission he would be burdened with for the rest of his life. Mugs stood motionless and expressionless, staring straight ahead. But his antenna eye quivered and rotated.

Then Mahkee made his request. He implored Dr. Shallot to take Mugs away from the planet and so relieve Mahkee of the great burden that had been placed upon him—and to make Mugs happy too, for his life would now be nothing but one misery after another.

"Golly," said Jack, "wouldn't that be something? Imagine taking Mugs to the White House to see the President!"

"He'd certainly be an attraction," said Mr. Warick. "And he'd be living proof of our findings. There are sure to be some people who won't believe our pictures and specimens. If we show them Mugs there won't be any room for argument."

"If they don't accept our word and our specimens," said Dr. Shallot, "then people will have to disbelieve us. It's out of the question to take Mugs from his planet."

As soon as he had spoken, Jack and Mr. Warick stopped their speculating, for they knew he was right.

"No," agreed Mr. Warick, "it just wouldn't work. Mugs couldn't live in the rich atmosphere of earth. Look at them, even now they're showing the effects of the increased pressure here in the ship."

Dr. Shallot spoke a long time to Mahkee, trying to explain that many hardships would have to be endured, and that an early death would result if Mugs left the underground. But Mahkee could not comprehend these explanations; he understood only that Dr. Shallot would not help him in his time of need. The scientist was helpless to assist Mahkee, so there was nothing for him to do but return to the underground with his charge. The crew watched them as the pair moved slowly over the landscape toward the entrance pit. Although the Martians did not show their feelings, the men knew that those two were forlorn, disappointed, and loath to take the steps that carried them back.

"Poor old Mugs," said Mr. Warick, "he certainly must hate to be banned, if he would rather go with us."

" 'Poor fellow' is right," said Dr. Shallot. "I'm afraid neither he nor Mahkee will be very happy. But then, Ahmon is no fool. He'll understand Mugs' reasons for acting the way he did, and maybe he'll straighten out the whole affair so everyone will be happy again."

He turned to the control panel.

"Let's hope Ahmon helps the two of them," said Mr. Warick. "We certainly can't do anything for them."

Dr. Shallot looked at the thermometers that registered the temperatures throughout the ship. "Looks as though we'll be able to take her off in about two hours," he said. "We'd better take a last tour around the ship."

Jack was checking through his personal locker to get the packet of soil that his mother had given him.

He handed the small, tightly stitched bundle to Dr. Shallot. "This is from my own back yard," he said. "It's soil that my mother gave me and asked me to leave on the planet." And as an afterthought, he said, "It's funny, she never questioned whether we'd get here at all. She just knew we would."

Dr. Shallot returned the packet to him. "You'd better take it out now, Jack. You'll be the last of the three of us to set foot on Mars."

When he reached the ground, Jack opened the packet and scattered the contents. He picked up a handful of the red powder that covered the surface of the planet and put it into the bag. He knew that this simple gift would mean more to his mother than gems or trinkets.

When he returned to the crew compartment, the take-off preparations were well under way.

"Give me a hand here, Jack," said Mr. Warick who was removing one of the bimag cases from the storage compartment. "We'll have to set this plutonium in the reactor."

When it was set in place, the escape hatch was battened down securely, and the atomic reactor was thrown into action. The plastic and silk webbing was stretched overhead to protect the instrument panel. Every bit of equipment was stowed away and fastened securely; each step was itemized in the flight manual that Dr. Shallot checked and rechecked.

Through all the preparations the crew felt an uncertainty which none of them expressed. Could the rocket do it? Could the *Lodestar* get away from the planet by using only its jets, independent of auxiliary rockets? It had never been done, and in spite of the opinions of earth's leading astronomers who said it could be done, there were learned skeptics who said it was impossible. The question would be answered soon.

The temperature dials were approaching maximum.

"Strap down," ordered Dr. Shallot.

As the men were getting into their seats and fastening their belts, the doctor briefed them for the last time.

"After zero minus ten there will be no talking. Keep as much air in your lungs and stomachs as you can. When I pull the throttle full open, we all fold into our seats. Is everything clear?"

"All clear," said Mr. Warick crisply.

"Suppose we pass out," asked Jack, "do we leave each other alone as we did before?"

"Right. No one is to unstrap until all have recovered, or until forty minutes have elapsed."

Dr. Shallot tightened the straps about his chest and stomach. He rechecked the controls and the lights that were blinking on the control panel. "When the second hand hits thirty, we'll drop all the rods out of the reactor," he said.

This meant that the atomic reactor would then operate at full speed.

The men threw back their heads and watched the hand move relentlessly toward thirty.

Twenty-seven, twenty-eight, twenty-nine, thirty. Dr. Shallot pushed a button. There was not a sound as the reactor went into full power. He watched the pressure gauge as it crept higher and higher. The minutes of waiting for it to reach take-off level seemed like hours. Finally it moved into the high position that caused a red light to blink rapidly.

"Ready, Don?" asked the doctor hoarsely.

"Right, Doctor."

"And you, Jack. All ready?"

"Ready," answered Jack. There was a lump in his throat and a weight in his stomach. His hands gripped the retaining belts with fingers of steel.

Dr. Shallot watched the dial that ticked off the seconds.

"Zero minus ten," he ordered in a calm, controlled voice.

The crew watched the dial. There was not a sound, although Jack could hear a roar inside his head like a pounding engine. The men were breathing in short gasps to retain air in their bodies. They could see, and almost feel, the seconds tick away.

" . . . minus six," they seemed to hear, "minus five, minus four, minus three, minus two, minus . . . "

The doctor threw the throttle and the men folded.

The ship raised and quivered. The three green lights

that indicated when the stilts were touching solid ground
blinked off and on as the *Lodestar* hesitated and strained
like a race horse pulling against the grip of its handler.

Moments later there was a deafening roar as the ship
rose straight into the air in a ball of white-hot fire. In seven
seconds the *Lodestar* was out of sight, and all trace of its
having been on the planet was erased. It had gone into
oblivion even faster than it had come out of it.

But even though no trace of the *Lodestar* remained
upon Mars, there were those who knew that this planet,
and all other planets of the solar system, would never be
the same, now that man had spanned the gulf that
separated them one from another.